Titles by

Francis B. Nyamnjoh
Stories from Abakwa
Mind Searching
The Disillusioned African
The Convert
Souls Forgotten
Married But Available
Intimate Strangers

Dibussi Tande
No Turning Back. Poems of Freedom 1990-1993
Scribbles from the Den: Essays on Politics and Collective Memory in Cameroon

Kangsen Feka Wakai
Fragmented Melodies

Ntemfac Ofege
Namondo. Child of the Water Spirits
Hot Water for the Famous Seven

Emmanuel Fru Doh
Not Yet Damascus
The Fire Within
Africa's Political Wastelands: The Bastardization of Cameroon
Oriki'badan
Wading the Tide
Stereotyping Africa: Surprising Answers to Surprising Questions

Thomas Jing
Tale of an African Woman

Peter Wuteh Vakunta
Grassfields Stories from Cameroon
Green Rape. Poetry for the Environment
Majunga Tok: Poems in Pidgin English
Cry, My Beloved Africa
No Love Lost
Straddling The Mungo: A Book of Poems in English & French

Ba'bila Mutia
Coils of Mortal Flesh

Kehbuma Langmia
Titabet and the Takumbeng
An Evil Meal of Evil
The Earth Mother

Victor Elame Musinga
The Barn
The Tragedy of Mr. No Balance

Ngessimo Mathe Mutaka
Building Capacity: Using TEFL and African Languages as Development-oriented Literacy Tools

Milton Krieger
Cameroon's Social Democratic Front: Its History and Prospects as an Opposition Political Party, 1990-2011

Sammy Oke Akombi
The Raped Amulet
The Woman Who Ate Python
Beware the Drives: Book of Verse
The Wages of Corruption

Susan Nkwentie Nde
Precipice
Second Engagement

Francis B. Nyamnjoh & Richard Fonteh Akum
The Cameroon GCE Crisis: A Test of Anglophone Solidarity

Joyce Ashuntantang & Dibussi Tande
Their Champagne Party Will End! Poems in Honor of Bate Besong

Emmanuel Achu
Disturbing the Peace

Rosemary Ekosso
The House of Falling Women

Peterkins Manyong
God the Politician

George Ngwane
The Power in the Writer: Collected Essays on Culture, Democracy & Development in Africa

John Percival
The 1961 Cameroon Plebiscite: Choice or Betrayal

Albert Azeyeh
Réussite scolaire, faillite sociale : généalogie mentale de la crise de l'Afrique noire francophone

Aloysius Ajab Amin & Jean-Luc Dubois
Croissance et développement au Cameroun : d'une croissance équilibrée à un développement équitable

Carlson Anyangwe
Imperialistic Politics in Cameroun: Resistance & the Inception of the Restoration of the Statehood of Southern Cameroons
Betrayal of Too Trusting a People: The UN, the UK and the Trust Territory of the Southen Cameroons

Bill F. Ndi
K'Cracy, Trees in the Storm and Other Poems
Map: Musings On Ars Poetica
Thomas Lurting: The Fighting Sailor Turn'd Peaceable / Le marin combattant devenu paisible
Soleil et ombre

Kathryn Toure, Therese Mungah Shalo Tchombe & Thierry Karsenti
ICT and Changing Mindsets in Education

Charles Alobwed'Epie
The Day God Blinked
The Bad Samaritan
The Lady with the Sting

G. D. Nyamndi
Babi Yar Symphony
Whether losing, Whether winning
Tussles: Collected Plays
Dogs in the Sun

Samuel Ebelle Kingue
Si Dieu était tout un chacun de nous ?

Ignasio Malizani Jimu
Urban Appropriation and Transformation: bicycle, taxi and handcart operators in Mzuzu, Malawi

Justice Nyo' Wakai
Under the Broken Scale of Justice: The Law and My Times

John Eyong Mengot
A Pact of Ages

Ignasio Malizani Jimu
Urban Appropriation and Transformation: Bicycle Taxi and Handcart Operators

Joyce B. Ashuntantang
Landscaping and Coloniality: The Dissemination of Cameroon Anglophone Literature

Jude Fokwang
Mediating Legitimacy: Chieftaincy and Democratisation in Two African Chiefdoms

Michael A. Yanou
Dispossession and Access to Land in South Africa: an African Perspevctive

Tikum Mbah Azonga
Cup Man and Other Stories
The Wooden Bicycle and Other Stories

John Nkemngong Nkengasong
Letters to Marions (And the Coming Generations)
The Call of Blood

Amady Aly Dieng
Les étudiants africains et la littérature négro-africaine d'expression française

Tah Asongwed
Born to Rule: Autobiography of a life President
Child of Earth

Frida Menkan Mbunda
Shadows From The Abyss

Bongasu Tanla Kishani
A Basket of Kola Nuts
Konglanjo (Spears of Love without Ill-fortune) and Letters to Ethiopia with some Random Poems

Fo Angwafo III S.A.N of Mankon
Royalty and Politics: The Story of My Life

Basil Diki
The Lord of Anomy
Shrouded Blessings

Churchill Ewumbue-Monono
Youth and Nation-Building in Cameroon: A Study of National Youth Day Messages and Leadership Discourse (1949-2009)

Emmanuel N. Chia, Joseph C. Suh & Alexandre Ndeffo Tene
Perspectives on Translation and Interpretation in Cameroon

Linus T. Asong
The Crown of Thorns
No Way to Die
A Legend of the Dead: Sequel of *The Crown of Thorns*
The Akroma File
Salvation Colony: Sequel to *No Way to Die*
Chopchair
Doctor Frederick Ngenito

Vivian Sihshu Yenika
Imitation Whiteman
Press Lake Varsity Girls: The Freshman Year

Beatrice Fri Bime
Someplace, Somewhere
Mystique: A Collection of Lake Myths

Shadrach A. Ambanasom
Son of the Native Soil
The Cameroonian Novel of English Expression: An Introduction

Tangie Nsoh Fonchingong and Gemandze John Bobuin
Cameroon: The Stakes and Challenges of Governance and Development

Tatah Mentan
Democratizing or Reconfiguring Predatory Autocracy? Myths and Realities in Africa Today

Roselyne M. Jua & Bate Besong
To the Budding Creative Writer: A Handbook

Albert Mukong
Prisonner without a Crime: Disciplining Dissent in Ahidjo's Cameroon

Mbuh Tennu Mbuh
In the Shadow of my Country

Bernard Nsokika Fonlon
Genuine Intellectuals: Academic and Social Responsibilities of Universities in Africa

Lilian Lem Atanga
Gender, Discourse and Power in the Cameroonian Parliament

Cornelius Mbifung Lambi & Emmanuel Neba Ndenecho
Ecology and Natural Resource Development in the Western Highlands of Cameroon: Issues in Natural Resource Managment

Gideon F. For-mukwai
Facing Adversity with Audacity

Peter W. Vakunta & Bill F. Ndi
Nul n'a le monopole du français : deux poètes du Cameroon anglophone

Emmanuel Matateyou
Les murmures de l'harmattan

Ekpe Inyang
The Hill Barbers

JK Bannavti
Rock of God *(Kilán ke Nyùy)*

Godfrey B. Tangwa (Rotcod Gobata)
I Spit on their Graves: Testimony Relevant to the Democratization Struggle in Cameroon

Henrietta Mambo Nyamnjoh
"We Get Nothing from Fishishing", Fishing for Boat Opportunies amongst Senegalese Fisher Migrants

Bill F. Ndi, Dieurat Clervoyant & Peter W. Vakunta
Les douleurs de la plume noire : du Cameroun anglophone à Haïti

Laurence Juma
Kileleshwa: A Tale of Love, Betrayal and Corruption in Kenya

Nol Alembong
Forest Echoes (Poems)

Marie-Hélène Mottin-Sylla & Joëlle Palmieri
Excision : les jeunes changent l'Afriaque par le TIC

Walter Gam Nkwi
Voicing the Voiceless: Contributions to Closing Gaps in Cameroon History, 1958-2009

John Koyela Fokwang
A Dictionary of Popular Bali Names

Alain-Joseph Sissao
(Translated from the French by Nina Tanti)
Folktales from the Moose of Burkina Faso

Folktales from the Moose of Burkina Faso

Alain-Joseph Sissao
(Translated from the French by Nina Tanti)

Langaa Research & Publishing CIG
Mankon, Bamenda

Publisher:
Langaa RPCIG
Langaa Research & Publishing Common Initiative Group
P.O. Box 902 Mankon
Bamenda
North West Region
Cameroon
Langaagrp@gmail.com
www.langaa-rpcig.net

Distributed outside N. America by African Books Collective
orders@africanbookscollective.com
www.africanbookscollective.com

Distributed in N. America by Michigan State University Press
msupress@msu.edu
www.msupress.msu.edu

ISBN: 9956-616-55-9

DISCLAIMER

The names, characters, places and incidents in this book are either the product of the author's imagination or are used fictitiously. Accordingly, any resemblance to actual persons, living or dead, events, or locales is entirely one of incredible coincidence.

Contents

Translator's Preface

The stories in this collection were not originally written, but spoken. The author, Alain Sissao, first listened to the tales before transcribing them into Moore and then into French.

In my English translation I have therefore made an attempt to retain the oral quality of the language which I found in Mr. Sissao's French version. I have kept the simplicity of the language, the frequent repetitions and colloquialisms, and have tried to resist making the stories sound more "scholarly." My hope is that the reader will listen to, as well as read the tales.

Why publish these stories in English? The current translation will help to introduce the English-speaking world to the very rich culture of the Moose people of Burkina Faso. The book should appeal to both general readers interested in African folktales and folklore, as well as to students at the secondary or university level. Anthropology or African Studies departments might find the collection valuable for their undergraduate programs. And, with its proverbs, jokes and songs, the book enriches our understanding of oral literature and should contribute to the growing interest in that field.

I wish to thank my colleagues at Santa Clara University for their help and for their kind endorsements. Special thanks go to Alain Sissao and Michael Kevane both of whose knowledge of Burkina Faso I depended on, and through whom I learned that translation is as much about culture as it is about language.

Nina Tanti
Santa Clara University
April 20, 2010

Foreword

When I first began my research on the oral literature of the Moose as a student at the University of Ouagadougou in 1986, I had no intention of creating a book of folktales. However, the project took form in 1998 when I entered the *Intitut des Sciences et des Sociétés* of the *Centre National de la Recherche Scientifique* in Burkina Faso. This allowed me to make the most of my field work and add to my corpus.

Over the years as I traveled throughout the region with my tape recorder, I listened to stories from all segments of the population.

This small volume contains a selection of texts which seemed to me the most significant to give readers an idea of the variety of the oral cultural heritage of the Moose.

In this enterprise, I received the generous support and encouragements of Daniel Barreteau, director of research at the IRD (*Institut français de recherche pour le développement*).

I would also like to thank my research colleagues for the interest they showed in my work, as well as Karthala publications, who helped me to publish these selected texts.

Finally, without the Moose storytellers from Ouagadougou, Tenkodogo, Ganzourgou, and from many other villages of the Moogo, this book would not exist. I wholeheartedly thank them for showing me a part of the rich oral literature of which they are the keepers.

Introduction

The Moogo

The region of the Moose[1] people (who are incorrectly referred to as "Mossi" in old literature) is called Moogo. It occupies the entire central zone of Burkina Faso, or about 63,500 square kilometers, making up one fifth of the country. The Moogo is subdivided into several kingdoms: Tenkodogo, Wagdgo, and Yaatinga, which correspond to the modern cities of Tenkodogo, Ouagadougou and Yatenga. It includes other districts and principalities such as Bulsa, Mané, Busuma, and Yako.

The kingdom located in the center of the region includes today's capital of Ouagadougou. It is here that the chief ruler of the Moose, the *moogo naaba*, resides.

The Moose have a high opinion of their way of life (*moogo*) which they consider the best of all possible worlds and which is in opposition to the life of the bush (*weeogo*). For a long time the Moose rejected outside influences by adhering to a fierce and warrior-like isolation. For them, a stranger is someone who cannot be understood within the context of traditional culture or the main religious beliefs. This perception explains to a certain extent their initial resistance to Islam and to other outside influences.

The Moose also differentiate between *moogo* and *dûnya*[2]. *Moogo* represents a geographical, cultural and religious entity while *dûnya* stands for the everyday world.

Several sayings and proverbs reflect this notion of *dûnya:*

Dûnya yaa raaga. A sâ kê a pa zaed yiib ye.

"Life in this world is like the market place. Once you enter, you are soon to leave."

---

1. Singular: A Moaaga.

2. Word of Arabic origin which etymologically designates this lowly world.

Dûnya yaa menem a pa zaed yiib ye.

"Life is like the dew at sunrise. It soon evaporates and disappears."

Dûnya yaa yugemde, a sâ n gâande, bi f pîndi zombe.

"The world is like a camel. When it's lying down, you should take the opportunity to climb onto its back."

Dûnya yaa belgr doogo.

"The world is a deceptive dwelling place"

Dûnya!...Ne fo me!

"What a world !.... Yes, but you are part of it!"

The general meaning of this last proverb is this: "Let us not be surprised at what happens to us, for we are all affected by life's circumstances."

God and the Ancestors

The social universe of the Moose grants an important role to the ancestors, who protect and preserve the values of the group. It is they who watch over the life of the community.

There does exist, nevertheless, a supreme God (*Wende*), who is responsible for all things in life: fate, good, and evil. However he is only accessible by way of the ancestors. Thus in traditional religion, the role assigned to the ancestors is one of asking, giving, and receiving. The typical Moaaga is extremely polite. He will first address the king, then go through those who lived on earth before him—his ancestors—when asking something of God.

The traditional Moaaga fears his ancestors more than God. He will more readily take God's name in vain ("For God's sake!"), than swear in the name of his dead father or in the name of the family spirits. This leads him to forgive more easily on behalf of his forefathers than on God's behalf. He will also relent in the name of his ancestor. But once he does swear by his ancestor, he will persevere to the end, for he would rather die than go back on his word.

The Family

The Moose possess a strong social structure that is based on the family (*buudu*). Within the family unit a child receives an education which values the collectivity. The Moose believe that friendship is a feeling that may end one day, whereas family ties are eternal. The *buudu* is comprised of the larger family of relatives on the father's side which protects the child and helps the child to grow. The father and mother represent the foundation to which the child owes respect and obedience.

The Moore Language

The term Moore designates both the language and the culture of the Moose people. Moore is spoken by over three million people in Burkina Faso as well as in the Ivory Coast and Ghana, two countries where the Moose have migrated. Moore also serves as the lingua franca between neighboring groups, such as the Bisa and Gurunsi.

The Moore language belongs to the Gur or Voltaic branch of the Niger-Congo family, of the phylum Niger-Kordofanien. Its spelling has been officially regulated.

The Griot, Keeper of the Traditional Word

In Moore, the word *bendre* (plural: *benda*) means both the calabash drum and the person of the griot, who is master of the Word. He holds the power of the Word and is the authority on the history of the region and the village.

The griot is thus skilled in the art of storytelling and has the gift of making the past come alive. He also knows how to guard the secrets of the kingdom. He occupies a special place in the courtyard, standing under a shelter known as *bendazande*. This shelter protects the drummers and particularly the calabash drummers from inclement weather.

The drummers protected by this shelter serve a very important purpose, for they act more as memory keepers than musicians. In particular, it was their job every morning to recite the royal genealogy, as well as the battle names.

The *bend-naba*, who commands the *benda* players, is the chief of all the griots. One of his principal contributions was to encourage warriors during combat. Consequently, he participated in all of the war campaigns.

Musical Instruments

The principal musical instruments of the Moose are the armpit drum (*lùnga*), the cylindrical drum (*gângâoogo*), the one-stringed violin (*ruudga*), the horn trumpet (*baorgo*), the flute (*wiiga*), the three-stringed lute (*koende*), the upside-down calabash, the maracas (*silsâka*), and the percussion rods (*keama*). However, the calabash drum (*bendre*) is without a doubt the most important instrument of all, and the one who plays it, also called *bendre*, receives the respect of all the other musicians. Indeed, he alone has the authority to inaugurate the funeral watches, for only he has the power to "call" the dead. And he is always the first to lead the singing in honor of the authorities. If there is one man with a delicate role to play, it is he, for he must be above all a good "servant" to the chief.

The Evening Storytellers

The sacred role of the *bendre* in the art of storytelling is complementary to the more secular role attributed to the evening storytellers. The latter are also considered specialists of the Word. Along with the singing griots, they too, pass on the ancestral Word.

During the evening gatherings, the storytellers impress upon the group models of Mooaga society to follow.

The folktale is the most appropriate form for teaching young children to express themselves, to structure their thoughts, and to reason.

As for the level of acquisition, it should be noted that stories portraying the more or less familiar animals will be taught to the group of youngest children (the *yanse*). The legendary gluttony and foolishness of Mba-Katré, the hyena, in contrast with the cunning and finesse of Mba-Soâmba, the hare, will especially interest children from 10-12 years old. The tales describing the origin of things, the reason for various taboos, the legitimacy of social functions and structures, as well as character flaws that need correcting, should be reserved for adolescents (*rasamba ou pugsadba*), who will go on to analyze them with the help of the ancestors, even after initiation.

Through the process of reformulation, the storytellers also integrate into their tales societal changes as well as any new concerns of the group. The tale provides the opportunity for a critical examination of evolving social customs.

Principal Narrative Forms

Long tales

The "long tales" (*soalm wogdo*) are made up of fictional narratives, cosmological legends, fables, and *chantefables*, fables that have verses which are sung. These are imaginary stories whose purpose is to entertain during the evening gatherings. Generally speaking, the characters portrayed are Mba-Soâmba, the hare, Mba-Katré, the hyena, Mba-Kuri, the tortoise, Mba-Kaôngo, the guinea-fowl, Mba-Bonyenga or Mba-Wéôg-Naba, the lion, Mba-Wobgo, the elephant, and so on. The hare normally plays tricks on the hyena. The "long tales" provoke laughter. Moreover, they teach all sorts of lessons (moral, philosophical, worldview, arithmetic…).

The serious narrative

The *kibare*[3] designates the "serious narrative." Unlike the fable, it is a type of enigmatic tale that poses important questions and elicits reflection, analysis, and meditation and from which lessons of wisdom can be learned. It is the kind of story that adults are fond of, especially the elderly. The "serious narrative" is to adults what the "long tale" is to children. The *kibare* is in general refined, and reflects a certain social realism. It develops a highly philosophic view of the human experience. The *kibare* presents itself under two angles: fiction and reality. It can be narrated in the daytime or in the evening, during the evening gatherings.

3. Word of Arabic origin, whose etymology signifies: "information, piece of news."

1

The Rooster and the Elephant

A rooster and an elephant were courting the same woman. The day came when they were to meet. Arriving at the home of his future wife the rooster said:

"If I ever come across the one who is courting the same woman as I am, I'll show him who's boss!"

After saying this he tore off his tail feathers and stuck them in the middle of a garbage heap. As soon as the rooster left, the elephant arrived. He asked:

"Where is my rival?"

He was told that he was just there, and that he had left his feathers. The elephant asked to see them. Upon seeing them, the elephant laughed. With his left hoof he stamped the ground. The footprint he made became a pond. And he said:

"The day I meet the rooster, I will show him what courage is!"

So they planned to meet twelve days later to determine who was the bravest and who would win the woman.

The rooster's supporters were the bee and the wasp. On his side, the elephant gathered together all the four-legged animals, and even the toads. Each of them got ready for the day of battle. No-Raôgo, the rooster, went to get two cans : one he filled with curdled milk and the other, with a reddish liquid he had obtained by crushing shea nuts.

On the day of the battle, the calao bird was the rooster's war chief. The elephant was the first to arrive. He asked the monkey to climb up into a Caicedrat tree[1] to see if his enemies were on their way. When the rooster saw the monkey in the tree, he asked a bird to go and strike him on the head with the can of milk.

The bird went and struck the monkey. The can broke and the milk spilled out all over the monkey's body. Those watching cried out in horror: the monkey's head had split open and his brains were spilling out!

But what the people thought was brains, was nothing but curdled milk. The monkey began cleaning himself off. The bird with the can full of the red liquid obtained from the shea nuts arrived and struck again. This time, everyone was sure it was over.

Meanwhile, the calao bird sang:

Zom bugum, n tabd bugum!
Zom bugum, n tabd bugum!
Climb onto the fire, stamp out the fire!
Climb onto the fire, stamp out the fire!

And the rooster took up the song:

Ked wum yangsee heee!
The deer are conquered!

The rooster and his followers were now walking towards the meeting place. The bees said to the rooster:

"Leave them to us! We will sting them and see what happens. If we aren't able to kill them off, the other flying insects will come help us out."

Before he knew it, the elephant was stung all over, in his trunk, in his ears, between his toes… The bees stung him so much that he couldn't keep still. He realized there were

1. *Khaya senegalensis* (Meliaceae), *kuka* in Moore.

too many of them. He decided to flee. All the four-legged animals followed him. The rooster's followers chased them off, singing:

Zom bugum, n tabd bugum!
Zom bugum, n tabd bugum!
Zom bugum, n tabd bugum!
Zom bugum, n tabd bugum! …

In their rush to escape, the four-legged animals trampled the toads and the chickens swallowed them up.

And this is how flying insects won the woman for the rooster.

2

The Election of the Imam

One day, all the animals of the bush gathered together to elect an imam. To be elected, one had to prove to be cleverer than the rest. The meeting took place at the edge of a pond. It was decided that the one who finished washing himself first would be elected.

So one by one, the animals took their kettle, drew water, and began to wash themselves as fast as they could. Everyone was excited, except for the hyena, who sat calmly at the edge of the pond. The others asked him:

"Hyena, don't you want to become imam?"

The hyena said nothing but continued watching them until they had all finished washing. Then they got up to recite verses from the Koran. They had hardly begun when the hyena suddenly jumped into the pond crying out:

"*Alaahu akbaru*[1]! If it's not too much, I don't think it's insufficient. You washed your feet and your hands, you dried your ears and scrubbed your head, and as for me, I simply washed myself. Between the one who washed himself and the one who washed without cleaning his chest and his torso, who is the first to finish?"

It was unanimously decided that the hyena should be named imam.

---

1. "God is the greatest!" in Arabic.

Ever since that day, when the hyena leaves the bush to go to the village, he spends his time reciting verses from the Koran. There are verses he recites in such a way that even if you are sitting in a group, the hyena will come up and take what he wants from right under your nose and go back the way he came, without anyone saying a thing.

The day the hyena was named imam, this power was granted to him at the same time.

3

What Happened?

The expression, "What happened?" has an origin. No-Raôgo, the rooster, had organized a "work party"[1]. Everyone came to help him cultivate his field.

When the work was going full speed and everyone was starting to get hungry, the rooster decided to go get the workers something to eat. On the way, he came across Mba-Wibga, the white hawk[2]. The bird struck at him with his beak, but as luck would have it, missed him. The rooster hid under a cooking pot.

After waiting in vain for the rooster to return, Bumpoaka, the lizard, decided to go see what was happening. "What happened? The rooster hasn't come back yet," he wondered.

On the way, he met the white hawk who attacked him as well. He hid in the trunk of a tree. The bird flew onto one of the branches of the tree and stayed there. From his hiding place the rooster glanced up occasionally, and each time he saw that the bird was still perched on his branch.

Nighttime came, the bird flew away, and the rooster could finally come out, as well as the lizard. They met up and the rooster asked:

"What happened?"

---

1. *Sosoaaga* in the Moore language.

2. Small bird of prey, *Elanus caeruleus* (Accipitridae).

The lizard also asked:

"What happened?"

And the rooster said again:

"What happened?"

And the rooster replied:

"Don't you see? I went to look for some food under a cooking pot!"

The lizard also explained his case:

"As for me, I went looking for you; I was attacked, and I hid in the trunk of a tree. I have just now come out."

That is the origin of the expression *Maana waana*? "What happened?"

4

The Warthog and the Lion

The warthog and the lion did not get along. It was even said that the warthog was not easy to beat. Bon-Yênga, the lion, ended up taking offense at this:

"What? I am called king of the bush and someone in this bush dares to say that he is not easy to beat?"

The day came when they were to meet. It was quite a confrontation.

Réôgo, the warthog, began to dig up roots with his teeth. Meanwhile, the lion tore out grass[1] with his claws.

When they met up, God gave the lion courage and he was able to catch the warthog. He grabbed him, but he escaped; the warthog bolted and the lion charged after him. The warthog went and hid down a hole.

The hyena was put in charge of guarding the hole.

Meanwhile, they started digging.

Another warthog was brought over in order to dig out the one hidden in the hole.

The hare, informed of the news, went and got some salt and put it in his sack.

While they were digging, the hare said:

"Wait a minute; I will go inside to see if he's still there."

Inside the hole he found the warthog and told him:

---

1. Grasses whose straw is used to make mats.

"You see, they are waiting outside to catch you. Take this salt and put it in your mouth! When the one who is digging gets close to you, spit the salt into his eyes. If you spit the salt into his eyes, he will fall down and you can get away."

The hare came out and announced that the warthog was still far down the hole.

The warthog at the bottom of the hole put the salt into his mouth, and finding it tasty, swallowed it.

When the first warthog got very close to the second, the hare thought he was going to spit out the salt. But nothing happened. He asked again to go down into the hole and see.

Once inside, he asked:

"What did you do with the salt? Didn't you put it in your mouth so that you could spit it out?"

"I tasted it and since it tasted good, I swallowed it!"

"You swallowed it? Then you're going to die!"

"If you give me some more, I won't swallow it again!"

The hare gave him some more and left.

The warthog kept the salt in his mouth and waited. When the warthog who was digging got close, his eyes wide open, the one inside the hole spit the salt into his face and the other fell flat on his back. The hare then said:

"Where is the lion? Look! You told this warthog to dig a hole to catch your enemy, and he swallowed him! See! He's lying on his back, laughing!"

Meanwhile, the warthog who had been digging had very sore eyes, and the other was running off into the bush.

This is how the hare saved the first warthog. But the war between the lion and the warthog is not over yet. That is why when the lion kills a warthog, he tears off his feet and abandons him.

5

A Year Without Criticizing

There was once a year when it was forbidden to criticize others. If anyone ever criticized another, he would die.

One day, Mba-Soâmba, the hare, went to the side of the road. He climbed onto a large rock and began to pull weeds. Those passing by greeted him. When they greeted him, he answered:

"We have decided to cultivate this rock in order to grow eggplants."

The passersby nodded in agreement, but then added:

"We are not supposed to criticize others, but no one can cultivate a rock in order to grow eggplants!"

The one who said this died instantly.

As for the hare, he gathered the meat from the dead animal and ate it with his wife and children. This is how he nearly killed off all the animals in the bush.

Meanwhile Kângo, the guinea hen, understood why the hare was so happy and she swore to make him pay. She prepared some shea butter, filled a plate with it, and walked over to the hare. She greeted him. The hare answered:

"We have decided to cultivate this rock in order to grow eggplants!"

"And we have decided to go to Silmisê[1] to get our hair done," said the guinea hen.

"We are not supposed to criticize others, but we're going to do it anyway! How can someone with such a bald head get her hair done?" asked the hare.

At these words, the hare dropped dead.

This time, it was the guinea hen's turn to pick him up.

1. The quarter where the Peuls live.

6

The Hare and the Village Chief

A village chief had a grape tree[1]. No one was allowed to eat its fruit, but the hare decided to try everything he could.

So he went to see the chief and told him that a strong, dangerous wind was coming. "There is nothing that the wind cannot blow away, except for trees," he told him.

When he heard this, the chief told the hare to tie him to his grape tree so that the wind could not blow him away. No sooner said than done. The hare attached the chief firmly to his grape tree.

Once the chief was tied up, the hare used him as a ladder so he could climb into the tree. When he was up there, he ate the fruit; he ate until he was full. Then, he invited all the other animals to come and eat some, telling them that the chief had given the order that day to eat the fruit of his tree.

All those who came used the chief as a ladder to climb up. After eating their fill, they used him again to climb down, and off they went.

Meanwhile, the chief happened to notice some termites that were crawling by. He begged them to save him. He told them of his misfortune. The termites agreed to come chew the rope, and they delivered him. Very satisfied, the chief told the termites to come to the palace the following day. He promised them that he would have the animals killed and would cook them up for the termites.

---

1. *Lannea microcarpa* (Anacardiaceae). This tree has bunches of purplish-black ellipsoidal drupes. Its fruit is edible and very much appreciated.

While the chief was speaking to the termites, the hare, hidden in a bush, heard everything. The next day, the hare got all dressed up, hid his large ears, and went to the chief's for the feast. No one recognized him. He was shown into the house where he was served a hearty meal. He ate his fill. But as he ate, he didn't throw away the bones. He hid them in his bag.

When he had finished eating, he lay down to rest. He fell asleep and a glimpse was seen of one of his long ears. He was discovered. The chief was informed that it was the hare who was there, and not a termite. The noise woke the hare. Realizing that he had been unmasked, he jumped outside and began to run. The dogs were sent after him. But when they drew near, he threw them the bones which he had saved in his bag. They abandoned their chase and went back for the bones.

The hare went off. He covered himself with mud and stopped under a tree. A dog noticed him and asked:

"Is that Mba-Walga, the antelope?"

The hare said:

"Yes!"

The dog asked him if by any chance he had seen the hare. He told him that as a matter of fact that was him over there, causing all that dust to rise in the distance.

The dog took up his chase once more and the hare returned safely home.

7

The Chief's Daughter

A chief had a daughter. He wanted to marry her to a clever man. So he came up with this challenge:

"The one who brings me the brain of a genie, some milk from a she-buffalo, and the tendon of a tortoise, will have my daughter in marriage."

The hare thought these things would be easy to obtain, so he set off in search of them. In the bush he found a she-buffalo that was looking for some monkey bread[1] for her children. The hare greeted her and said:

"Since you are so strong, all you need to do is back up, get a running start, then charge into the baobab. That way, the fruit will fall and each of us will take some for our children."

No sooner said than done: the she-buffalo gathered up speed and charged into the baobab tree. Her horns sank deep into the trunk. The hare went to fetch his calabash bowl and began to milk the she-buffalo, saying:

"It is said that no one can milk a she-buffalo, but we know how to do it."

He filled his calabash.

---

1. The quarter where the Peuls live.

The hare continued his search. He met the genie *kinkirga*, and asked him:

"Dear *kinkirga*, can you do a summersault on top of a rock?"

The latter said no.

He told him that in that case, all he needed to do was to follow him to learn how.

He led the little genie up to the top of the rock. He did the first summersault to show him how it was done. The genie wanted to imitate him, but he struck his head against the rock and broke his skull. The hare collected his brain and continued on his way.

He arrived in the middle of the bush and said:

"Hey! All you the inhabitants of the bush, come, all of you! For the sky said that you have taken his egg away, and he asks that you give it back!"

All of the animals of the bush gathered around the hare.

"Since you cannot give the sky his egg back," he told them, "all you have to do is to go up and apologize to him."

The hare told the animals to climb on top of one another.

"Since the tortoise has a shell," he added, she has to be on the bottom so that all the other animals can climb on top of her."

So the tortoise lay down, and the elephant as well as the other animals climbed onto her back. Knowing that the tortoise could no longer move, the hare began to sever the tendon of one of her back legs. Surprised, the tortoise asked:

"Who is cutting off one of my tendons?"

The hare replied:

"Listen, everyone! Take up the song which the tortoise has just begun to sing !"

And the others started to sing in chorus:

Saaree geele !

When he had finished cutting the tendon, the hare left them, one on top of the other, and ran to the chief's house. He gave him the buffalo milk, the genie's brain, and the tendon from the hind leg of a tortoise.

In return, the chief gave him his daughter in marriage.

8

The Man and the Wild Animals

The wild animals decided to do everything they could to become more intelligent and stronger than man. They found it unfair that the bush was full of animals such as the elephant and the gazelle, and that in spite of their strength none of them could defeat man, who remained the most powerful.

They decided to send one of their own to where man lived to ask him a few questions: How is it that he has two feet and that his strength is not worth the gazelle's, yet he is more intelligent than those who have four feet? How did that come about?

The lion was elected to go question man. He started out. At the entrance to the village he found a man who was looking for some termites for his chickens. He greeted him and the latter responded in kind. He told him he had come on behalf of all the animals of the bush, and that he wanted to see him. The man asked him the reason for his visit. He told him that he had been sent to ask him the following question:

"How is it that you have only two feet and yet you are the strongest? What is your secret?"

The man let him finish, greeted him, and told him he had done well to come. He went on:

"However, you should have told me you were coming so that I could have gathered together all the intelligences, and brought them here. At the moment, I have only one here with me. But that's all right. I will show it to you. You will come back later so that I can show you the rest."

Satisfied, the lion thanked him and accepted his proposal. He followed the man. The latter tore off several strips of *bâgna*[1] bark.

Afterwards, they came upon a tree. The man asked the lion to lean up against it. He willingly accepted. The man tied him tightly to the tree. When he had finished, he said:

"They sent you to discover our secret so that they themselves could become stronger than us?"

"Yes," said the lion.

"I will show you just one intelligence," said the man.

He picked up the hoe he had been using to dig in the termite hole, and pretended to hit him. The lion cried out and the man said to him:

"Are you crying? Patience! It's coming!"

He took his knife and pretended to slit the lion's throat. The later yelled even louder.

"Listen," the man told him, "If I did not fear God, you would be my prey. On the other hand, if I kill you, there will be no one to go and tell the other animals what man is. This is why you are still alive. However, I do have to make you suffer somewhat; that way when you return to the bush you will tell them to respect man because, apart from God, man fears nothing."

He took up his knife again, made a mark on the lion's back, and cut off his tail before setting him free.

The lion ran off and went to find the other animals, who were busy playing. When they saw him they said:

"Here is the bold one!"

---

1. A shrub whose fibrous bark is torn off in strips and used in making rope.

They were all happy. When he was in the midst of them, the elephant approached:

"How did you manage to see him? What did he say?"

The lion remained silent.

Then he told them:

"Be patient, I am going to rest now because I cannot speak for the moment. Let me catch my breath."

After resting, he told them:

"You ask me how it went? Well! Didn't I leave here with a tail?"

And they replied, yes. He went on:

"Look at my back! Where is my tail?…Listen, I am telling you now. If you see man walking, run until your claws are gone because he is not someone to be trifled with! Today, if he had wanted to, I'd be done for, that's for sure!"

9

The Hyena and the Hare

Mba-Katré, the hyena, and Mba-Soâmba, the hare, were friends.

There had been such a famine that no one had anything to eat.

So the hare made an offer to the hyena. He proposed that each one of them sell his mother in order to buy some millet.

At his house, the hare tied his mother up with an old decaying rope. The hyena tied his up with a thick rope which was impossible to cut.

So, they both took their mothers to the market.

Meanwhile, the hare said to his mother:

"Your rope is an old one with no strength left to it. You must escape and run home. I will meet up with you there."

At the market, the hyena did in fact sell his mother and buy some millet, whereas the hare's mother ran away. The hyena loaded his millet onto his donkey and set out for home.

He saw the hare lying in the middle of the road as if he were dead. He said, "Oh no !" while continuing on his way.

A little further on he saw another hare. An idea came to him:

"I will turn around to pick up the hares that I saw so that I can prepare a good sauce with them." He left his donkey loaded up with millet and went to get the hares.

When the hare saw that the hyena had abandoned his donkey with the millet in order to go back and get the hares, he emptied out all of the millet and filled the sacks with sand. He took the millet home for his family.

The hyena did not find any hares, and continued on his way. Entering the village, the hyena called to his wife to throw out her bad sauce because he had brought some millet. His wife threw out her sauce and brought her basket to get some millet. When they untied the sacks they saw that they were full of sand. They left them and ran to get the sauce which had been thrown away behind the compound.

After that, the famine nearly caused the hyena's family to starve to death.

One day, the hyena's wife went to get some fire at the home of the hare's wife. She found her with her children, eating. The hare's wife let her have a bit of porridge[1] before giving her a few burning coals. On the way home the hyena's wife put out the fire by urinating on it, and turned around. She was again given some porridge. She ate some once more, and repeated her ruse.

But the third time the hare's wife refused to give her any, and said:

"The reason you are going to starve is because your husband is a fool."

---

1. *Sagbo* in Moore. Dish made from millet or corn flour, eaten daily by the Moose. It is eaten with a sauce made with okra or sorrel leaves.

10

The Dance of the Wild Animals

One day, the wild animals received a bull as a gift. They decided to organize a competition where the winner would get the bull. The competition consisted of dancing in order to raise as much dust as possible. The place they chose was a huge clearing where the ground was perfectly packed.

The big animals were the first contestants: elephants and buffaloes danced and danced, but none of them could raise any dust since the ground in the clearing was so firmly packed.

Meanwhile the hare, hiding, watched them while thinking of a way to win the competition and the bull at the same time.

He left his house and had a great big pair of trousers sewn, which he filled up with ashes. He was careful to tie the bottoms of the trouser legs.

When his turn came, he danced vigorously; meanwhile, using a ruse, he untied one of the legs of his huge pair of trousers and let a cloud of dust escape. The spectators began to cheer:

"Mba-Soâmba is the one who will get the bull! He is indeed the best dancer!"

This is how the hare won the bull.

11

The Friendship between the Hare and the Dog

Mba-Soâmba, the hare, and Mba-Bâga, the dog, were true friends. But one day the hare left the dog and went to make friends with the hyena. His strategy was this: one day he would chat in the dog's yard, the next day he would chat in the hyena's yard. He repeated this trick for a long time so that one day, the dog asked him:

"Mba-Soâmba, will everything turn out all right? You come to my house one evening; the next day, you are at the hyena's. Won't you one day say bad things about us?"

But the hare assured him that everything was fine, that there was no friction between them.

One day, the hare went to find the dog and asked him to accompany him to the funeral of a member of his wife's family. It so happens that the road which led to the hare's in-laws passed through the hyena's field. Worried, the dog told the hare:

"I wouldn't mind accompanying you to the funeral, but you see the road to the village cuts through the hyena's field, and you know that the hyena and I are enemies. I would like to come with you but I am sorry; in these conditions it's impossible."

The hare was not discouraged in the least and made the dog this offer:

"On the day of the journey I will bring a deep basket for you to hide in. What's more, I will carry you across the hyena's field."

On the day of departure, the dog put on a large, long-sleeved robe and a bonnet, and climbed into the basket. As planned, the hare carried him across the hyena's field.

It was sowing season. The hyena and his wife were in the process of sowing when the two friends passed by. When the hare was close to the hyena and his wife, he left the road and started to walk across the seedbeds.

The hyena commanded him to get back on the road.

So he returned to the road and moved a ways off. Then, once more he trampled the hyena's field, who again insisted that he leave his field.

Then the hare told the hyena that in that case he would lay his basket on the ground so that the hyena could come see for himself if anyone was able to carry such a heavy load without zig-zagging back and forth.

No sooner said than done. He emptied the contents of the basket in front of the hyena and his wife. The dog took off running and the hyena and his wife chased after him.

In his rush, the dog lost everything he was wearing. He arrived home with no robe or bonnet.

Luckily, he survived.

This is why it is recommended that everyone watch out for bad friends.

If you have a friend who gets along with your enemy, it is better to leave him.

12

The Hare and the Hyena

One day, the hare's child became ill. The hare went to consult a diviner. After the visit the diviner advised him to make a sacrifice to the mountain.

The hare collected the offerings: honey, fried dough, kola nuts. He went to talk to the mountain and gave him these things. His child was cured.

Once the child was better he still had to sacrifice a hyena to the mountain in order to show his gratitude. But how was one to get a hyena?

The hare went back to the diviner. The latter again asked for a sacrifice which the hare made.

He also needed millet beer for the sacrifice. The hare asked his wife to prepare some. Late that night, as the hare and his wife chatted while watching the fire under the pot of beer, the hyena passed by. She heard talking and saw the fire. She decided to take a look. Coming up the walk she asked the hare:

"Mba-Soâmba, why aren't you in bed so late at night? And this big fire here....."

"I have to make a sacrifice for tomorrow and this is why I am preparing some millet beer," replied the hare. "Do you see those chickens and that goat grouped together over there? All of that is for the sacrifice."

"If it's all right, may I come with you?" asked the hyena.

---

1. Literally: "squatting like a scatterbrain," nickname given to the hyena by the hare.

"Of course, but we must leave as soon as the cock crows. Come back then, and we'll leave together," said the hare.

The hyena went back home, but she was so impatient she couldn't get to sleep. She went and found a stick which she used to force the roosters to sing.

She went to see the hare and told him that the cocks had already crowed. The hare replied that it wasn't even daylight yet. He told her to go home and come back when the sun was up.

When she returned home, the hyena hung a clay pot up in a tree and lit a fire inside. She went back to the hare's place and said that the sun was beginning to rise. The hare replied that it was still too early. He told her to return home and wait for daylight.

She returned home.

Still impatient, she lit the bush on fire and ran to the hare's house to tell him that it was daytime. The hare told her to go home and come back a little later.

The hyena went to wait for sunrise behind the hare's compound.

The hare filled his jug with millet beer, put his goats on a lead, and swung the chickens onto his shoulder. The hyena took the jug of millet beer and dragged the goat up the mountain.

Once he arrived on the mountain, the hare said:

"Mountain, I came to beg you to cure my son and told you that if he got better, I would offer you a goat, some chickens, some millet beer as well as a *roãb-yiurgã*[1]. Today I have brought everything. But, Mountain, help me so that she won't refuse to do what I'm going to say."

The hyena was sitting down, and she didn't know that she was the one whom the hare had nicknamed *roãb-yiurgã* !

The hare began cutting the chickens' throats and said to the hyena:

"Isn't it wasteful to spill the chickens' blood on the ground?"

The hyena agreed. He went on:

"I'm going to slit the goat's throat. Since she has more blood than a chicken, why don't you lie down and open your mouth to drink it up?"

So she lay down and opened her mouth.

"Don't worry if you feel something warm," the hare told her, "it's just the heat from the knife, that's all."

The hare lay the goat down next to the hyena, telling the latter to shut her eyes so that the goat's blood wouldn't get into them. She closed them. The hare didn't touch the goat, but cut the hyena's throat instead. Before she even realized it, the hare had cut her throat! She struggled in vain, and died.

The hare went and found his goat and cut its throat.

This is how the mountain was satisfied and the hare's child was cured.

Everyone must be able to restrain himself, for gluttony does not honor man.

13

The Hare and the Hawk

The hare and the hawk were friends. There came a great famine. It was very difficult to find anything to eat.

The hare went to see the hawk that was on top of a tree and asked him to come down so they could discuss ways to help each other, in order to escape the famine. The hawk told him that he was so hungry that if he came down, he would not have the strength to fly back up into the tree again. But the hare insisted. He told him he had some bulls and that he would give him one for food.

The hawk accepted and came down from the tree. The hare did indeed kill a bull for the hawk and his family. Another day, the hare called the hawk and said:

"Come, together we will figure out how to get something to eat; if not, it won't be easy. I am going to make a drum; I'll go out into the bush and call together all the animals so that you and I can find a way to defeat the famine. When all the animals are here, you will light fires all over and then fly down and pick me up. That way, they will all be burned and we will be able to pick them up and eat them."

The hawk accepted. The hare struck his drum and gathered together all of the animals. The hawk did what the hare had asked him to do. The fire killed many animals. The hare and the hawk collected them and divided them up. Each one took his share home to his family.

One day, the hyena went to get fire at the hare's house. When she arrived, she saw a chunk of meat. The hare gave her a bit of it. The next day, the hyena went again to get some fire and the hare gave her a little more of the meat.

Then, the hyena told the hare to meet her behind the house because she had something to tell him. The hare came and the hyena grabbed him; she told him to show her where he had found all that meat, or else she wouldn't let him go.

The hare told her:

"It's simple; I made friends with the hawk: I killed some bulls for him, and in return he helped me burn the wild animals."

After hearing this, the hyena decided to become friends with the hawk. So she went to see him. The latter saw no problem becoming friends with the hyena in exchange for a bull.

But the hyena didn't have a bull to give the hawk. One day, she made him an offer:

"I am going to call all the animals of the bush together with my drum. When they get here, come and light fires all around. They will die and I'll have something to eat."

Unfortunately, she did not tell the hawk to come and get her after he had lit the fires.

At the sound of the drum, all the animals gathered together. When the hawk saw they were all there he set fire to the bush and disappeared. The hyena didn't know where to go. She and the other animals burned to death in the fire. The hare came and picked them up.

This is why we say that it is good to be strong, but you must also be clever, for strength alone is not enough.

14

The Wild Billy Goat and the Dog

One day the wild billy goat and the dog went fishing in a pond. While they were emptying the water from the pond[1], the hyena arrived and said to them:
"Dear billy goat, may I help you?"
She exchanged places with the billy goat and said:

Ko kaadb riibo
koom põg riibo;
ko kaadb riibo
koom põg riibo!
Those who empty the water
are to be eaten;
what is in the water
is to be eaten!

But the dog said to her:

"Dear hyena, do you know what *kalgem-kalgem*[2] is?"

The hyena said no.

The dog stopped emptying the water and went for a walk before returning to his work.

Meanwhile, the hyena went on humming her song:

Ko kaadb riibo
koom põg riibo;

---

1. This is a traditional method of fishing in a pond.

2. "To snack"

ko kaadb riibo
koom põg riibo!
Those who empty the water
are to be eaten;
what is in the water
is to be eaten !

The dog asked her again:

"Dear hyena, do you know what *vilem vilem*[3] is?"

The hyena said no.
The dog got up, went for a walk, and came back.
As they went on with their work, the dog asked her:
"Dear hyena, do you know what '*'to-risgo*[4] is?"
The hyena said no.

The dog fled and the hyena ordered him to come back, in vain. The dog was already far away. The hyena went off after him.

When they were gone, the wild billy goat went into the pond, covered himself with mud, and sat upon the edge.

The hyena chased after the dog, but she could not catch him. She returned to the pond where she found the billy goat. She greeted him, and asked:

"Have you come to fish?"

The billy goat said no, before adding:

"I only eat meat of the hyena!"

---

3. "To turn back."

4. "To escape."

And the hyena replied:

"Oh, really? How convenient, for I am a hyena! Wait! I'll show you how the turtledove walks, and I'll be right back!"

The hyena backed away and took off running.

The wild billy goat washed himself off and returned home.

15

The Hare and the Lion

One day, the hare set fire to the bush. Unfortunately, the fire reached the lion's children.

The lion promised to give a buffalo to the one who had set fire to the bush. The hare went to inform the hyena about this.

"My dear hyena, the lion wants to see the one who burned the bush today, so that he can offer him a buffalo!"

The hyena went to find the lion:

"My dear lion, it appears you are looking for the one who set the bush on fire?"

The lion said yes.

The hyena said that she was the one.

The lion replied:

"Oh really? So it was you who set fire to the bush?"

The hyena continued to say yes.

So, the lion set off and asked her to follow him.

A little farther on the lion asked again:

"Who burned this place, here?"

"I'm the one who burned all of that," the hyena replied.

The lion continued his walk with the hyena.

A little farther on, the lion asked his question again:

"Who burned this place, here?"

"Didn't I already tell you that I am the one who burned the whole area?" said the hyena with some annoyance.

They kept walking.

When they came to a small tree called a *bagênd*[1], the lion asked her once more:

"Who burned this area?"

"I already told you that I am the one who burned all that you see," said the hyena.

The lion walked around the small tree behind which were his dead cubs. He asked the hyena:

"Who burned this area"?

"No, here, it wasn't me. The fires got mixed up. I'm not the one who set the fire here," said the hyena.

The lion seized her and cut off her paws.

Even today, when the lion finds a hyena he cuts off her paws; he doesn't kill her.

---

1. Shrub whose bark is used to make rope.

16

The Witch

A man had several daughters. Every time he came home, he noticed that one of them had disappeared. When he asked what had happened the others replied:

"When you left, an old woman came by. She offered to do our hair, and afterwards we noticed that one of us was missing."

A few days later the old woman returned to do the girls' hair. Another one disappeared.

Frustrated, the man went to get a grain basket and a knife. He told his daughters to climb into a tree that was in the middle of the courtyard.

"If the old lady asks you to come down, don't do it!" he told them.

Once the girls were up in the tree, the man took his knife and hid himself in the grain basket.

A few minutes later, the old woman arrived. She asked the girls where their father was. They told her he had gone out. She asked them to come down so that she could do their hair. The girls refused.

The man came out of his hiding place, and with one strike of his knife, cut open the belly of the old woman. The missing girls came tumbling out and the old woman vanished into thin air.

This is how it was discovered that she was, in fact, a witch and a *tenkugri*[1].

---

1. Literally, "alter or shrine." The Moose believe that certain people entrust their protection to a sacred place called "*tenkugri*," or "shrine."

17

If God Does Not Kill, the Chief Cannot Kill Either

One day, a hunter went out to hunt. It was already getting late, and he still had not found anything. He searched around in a bush where he discovered a hedgehog and her babies. He picked them up and put them in his bag.

The little hedgehogs began to cry. Their mother told them to stop crying, for "If God doesn't kill, the chief cannot kill either."

The hunter continued to look for game, with no luck. He didn't find anything else and turned around to go home.

On the way, he saw an antelope eating grass. He put down his bag in order to kill it.

The hedgehog and her babies took this opportunity to escape.

That is why the Moose have this proverb:

"If God did not kill, then the chief cannot kill either[1]."

---

1. The power held by the chief is inferior to divine protection.

18

The Terrible Child and the Birds

There was a woman who was sterile.

One day she went to a healer to get a cure for sterility. The healer told her to go home, while giving her the following piece of advice:

"Go prepare some porridge[1]. But when you are preparing it, if some falls onto your thigh do not wipe it off!"

Indeed, as she prepared some porridge a little bit of it fell onto her thigh. She didn't wipe it off. It became a pimple. The pimple swelled up and burst. A child came out of it. When the child came out, he asked his mother:

"Mother, do you know my name?"

She said no.

He asked his father, who also said no.

So then the child told them that his name was Kegenkargen-bîga-na-zengloanda[2]. He asked his father to fetch him an iron club. His father gave him one.

The child took his club and went out into the bush. He met another child as brave as he was. They became friends. They decided to build a cage where they would put all of the birds they killed.

---

1. Common dish made from millet or corn flour, *sagbo* in Moore.
2. In the hero's name, we recognize the word *biiga* which means "child."

After killing several of them, they noticed that the number of birds in the cage was getting smaller. So they put Warpîgsenkonba[3] in charge of standing watch. Soon afterwards, the latter saw a big hawk hovering in the sky. It came down and asked him:

"Do you want me to eat the meat or a person?"

Warpîgsenkonba told him to eat the meat, because there was a person and there was some meat.

The hawk swallowed the birds and left. The children insulted Warpîgsenkonba and called him good-for-nothing. Someone else was chosen to guard the birds. Soon afterwards the hawk returned and asked him:

"Do you want me to eat the meat or a person?"

This one also told him to eat the meat, because there was a person and there was some meat. The hawk swallowed the birds and left.

Kegenkargen-bîga-na-zengloanda was therefore forced to stay behind and guard the birds himself. The hawk came and said to him:

"Do you want me to eat the meat or a person?"

The child told him to eat a person because there was a person and there was some meat.

The hawk swallowed him, but he came back out through his anus and struck him with his club. The hawk swallowed him again. Once more he came back out through his anus and struck him with his club. This is how he finally succeeded in killing the hawk.

When he began to pluck the hawk's feathers, the feathers turned into birds which flew away.

It is the birds which came from these feathers that now fill the world.

---

3. Animal of the bush.

19

The Children and their Aunt

Some children had an aunt. She came to visit them and wanted to go back home. But this aunt was a witch. The children's mother wanted them to accompany her home. That is why she sang[1]:

-Yam-pîga "ten intelligences,"
Will you accompany your aunt?
-I am Yam-pîga,
But I will not accompany my aunt.
-Yam-wae "nine intelligences,"
Will you accompany your aunt?
-I am Yam-wae,
But I will not accompany my aunt.
-Yam-nî, "eight intelligences,"
Will you accompany your aunt?
-I am Yam-nî,
But I will not accompany my aunt.
-Yam-yopoe "seven intelligences,"
Will you accompany your aunt?
-I am Yam-yopoe,
But I will not accompany my aunt.
-Yam-yôbe "six intelligences,"
Will you accompany your aunt?
-I am Yam-yôbe,
But I will not accompany my aunt.
Yam-nu "five intelligences,"

1. The purpose of this song is to teach how to count backwards (from 10 to 1).

-I am Yam-nu,
But I will not accompany my aunt.
-Yam-nâse "four intelligences,"
Will you accompany your aunt?
-I am Yam-nâse,
But I will not accompany my aunt.
-Yam-tâbo "three intelligences,"
Will you accompany your aunt?
I am Yam-tâbo,
But I will not accompany my aunt.
Yam-yîbu "two intelligences,"
Will you accompany your aunt?
I am Yam-yîbu,
But I will not accompany my aunt.
Yam-yende "one intelligence,"
Will you accompany your aunt ?
I am Yam-yende,
And I will accompany my aunt.
So Yam-yende accepted to accompany her aunt.
She was asked to carry the aunt's basket.

After leaving the courtyard, right behind the compound the aunt rolled in an anthill and turned into a buffalo to devour Yam-yende. At the same moment, the latter also changed into a root near the basket. The aunt could not find Yam-yende. So, she went and rolled in the anthill and turned back into a human and asked the girl:

"Yam-yende, where have you gone?"

"When you changed into a buffalo to eat me, I changed into a root next to the basket."

The aunt said to her:

"Carry the basket!"

She took the basket and began to walk in front of her aunt. When the latter saw another anthill she rolled in it and turned into a buffalo. The child changed into a fly stuck to the basket. The aunt saw a root and tore it from the ground with all of her strength. When she had finished, she again went to the anthill and became a human again. Yam-yende also changed into a human. The aunt asked her again:

"Yam-yende, where did you go?"
"Well! When you turned into a buffalo to devour me I turned into a fly and I stuck to the basket."

The aunt said to her:

"Take the basket, let us go on."

Farther on, the aunt noticed an anthill. She rolled in it and changed into a buffalo to devour Yam-yende. She saw a fly stuck on the basket. She fought with it and killed it, then changed into a human. When she got up, she saw Yam-yende standing there. Stupefied, she asked her:

"Yam-yende, where did you get to?
When you changed into a buffalo to eat me, I changed into a needle and I stuck to the basket."

So the aunt asked for her basket back and told her to go home, for she was too clever for her.

20

The Orphan Girl

A woman had died leaving her young child with her husband's second wife. The second wife went to sow okra in the bush. The okra grew and was ready to harvest. The step-mother forced the orphan girl to go out into the bush to harvest the okra.

The little orphan girl got up. Crying, she went towards the okra field, singing:

Sî lengen lengen leende!
Sî lengen lengen leende!
My father had a second wife,
sî lengen lengen leende!
Who took her two okra plants,
sî lengen lengen leende!
She planted them on the road to Kadyoog,
sî lengen lengen leende!
She planted them on the road to Tagrima,
sî lengen lengen leende!
She ordered me to go and pick them,
sî lengen lengen leende!
Hoping that the wild animals would eat me,
sî lengen lengen leende!
Hoping that the genies would eat me,
sî lengen lengen leende!

She was chanting in this way when she met an old woman. The latter told her to keep singing so that she could dance.

The orphan girl obeyed. The old woman danced and was very pleased. So she said to the orphan girl to accompany her home. And she brought her home with her. Once at the house, she began to wash herself, then she asked the little orphan girl to scrub her back. The latter obeyed. After her bath, she asked the girl:

"Do you want me to make you some red sorghum porridge[1] or some corn porridge?"

She replied that at home she didn't even have any red sorghum porridge, let alone any corn porridge.

So, the old woman made her some corn porridge to eat. After eating, she went to bed.

The next day, the old woman called to her and said:

"Thrust your right hand into this!"

She inserted her right hand, and when she took it out again it was covered in gold, up to the arm.

The old woman told her to put her left hand in. When she brought it out, she had the same amount of gold as on the other. Then, the old woman gave her permission to go home.

When she got home, the step-mother's daughter told her mother that the orphan girl had arrived covered in gold. The step-mother said that the orphan girl couldn't have anything like that. Her jealous daughter assured her that it was in fact the case, and she declared that she too wanted to have as much wealth as the orphan girl.

The step-mother became angry and began beating her own daughter while ordering her to go harvest her okra.

---

1. Dish made from millet or corn flour, eaten daily by the Moose, *sagbo* in Moore.

The girl left crying and singing:

Wɛɛ wɛɛ yi yee!
Wɛɛ wɛɛ n kê yee![2]

She was chanting in this way when she met the old woman who took her home with her. In the evening the old woman wanted to take her bath and she called for her to scrub her back. The girl replied that she didn't want to ruin her hands on a back as rough as hers. The old woman was silent, and washed herself.

After her bath, she asked the child if she wanted her to make her some red sorghum porridge or some corn porridge. The girl answered that at home, she ate only corn porridge. The old woman got up to prepare her some red sorghum porridge.

When she had finished eating, the old woman asked her to thrust her right hand into a hole. When the girl inserted her right hand, a snake coiled around it. She took her hand out.

The old woman told her to thrust her left hand into another hole. When she put her left hand inside, a scorpion bit it and stuck to the hand she brought out of the hole.

The old woman told her to thrust her head into another hole. When she thrust her head inside, it came off.

This is why we should take care of orphans, and stay humble in life.

---

2. Song of lamentation.

21

Keep your Promises!

Some women went into the bush. During their walk, they were thirsty. Seeing a tree called Afzelia[1], they asked it to turn into water to that they could quench their thirst. The tree replied:

"If I become water for you to drink, what will you give me in exchange?"

One of the women promised a guinea hen. Another, a goat. A third promised a bull. A fourth promised to give him a donkey. A fifth one said that if he became water, she would give him her eldest daughter.

The tree accepted and turned into water. The women quenched their thirst.

All of the women who had promised the tree something kept their promise, except the one who had promised her daughter.

Tired of waiting, the tree decided to demand what he was owed. He sent the hawk *kõõâa* to the woman's house. He went and perched on a tree behind the woman's hut and sang:

Kõõvâa kõõâa!
The Afzelia sends me to tell you this:
the blood of the donkey came,
the blood of the chicken came,

---

1. *Kânkalgâ* in Moore. This tree has a nutritive role and some of its parts are used in traditional medicine.

the blood of the sheep came,
the blood of the goat came,
the blood of the guinea hen came,
but that of the person is late in coming!

The woman threw a stone at the bird, who flew away.

After leaving the woman, the bird saw the woman's eldest daughter, whose name was Ringalé, in the process of pounding millet for making *dolo.*[2] He approached and began to sing:

Ringalé, Ringalé,
Ringalé is drawing
the water for her funeral!
Don't worry, Ringalé!
Go to bed, Ringalé!
Nothing will happen to you!

Ringalé, too, began to sing:

Father, listen to a bird
who utters evil words!
Listen to a bird
who utters evil words.

And the father replied:

"It is a bird from ancient times, my daughter!"

Even though her father tried to reassure her, the daughter was convinced that the bird wanted her dead. She knew that it was the tree which had turned into a bird and that he had come to kill her.

---

2. Millet beer.

One day while Ringalé was pounding millet, the bird came again:

Ringalé, Ringalé!
Ringalé is grinding
the millet for her funeral!
Don't worry Ringalé!
Go to bed, Ringalé.
Nothing will happen to you!

The child, too, sang, to tell her mother and father.
Father, listen to a bird
who utters evil words!
Listen to a bird
who utters evil words!

Her father replied:

"It is a bird from ancient times, my daughter!"
The days passed, and the *dolo* was not ready on the day it was to be drunk.
The bird came back and began singing again:

Ringalé, Ringalé!
Ringalé is drinking
the dolo for her funeral!
Don't worry Ringalé!
Go to bed, Ringalé!
Nothing will happen to you!

Ringalé's father went into a rage and threw stones at the bird, who flew away. Then, he beat his wife and his daughter to death, thinking that this would make the bird leave him alone.
This is why we say that if someone makes a promise, he must keep it.

22

Poko and Raôgo[1]

A woman gave birth to twins in the bush. Their names were Poko and Raôgo.

The mother brought Poko home, while abandoning Raôgo in the bush.

A hawk came and found Raôgo in tears. Taking pity on the poor baby, he brought him to his nest where he raised him.

When he grew up, the first thing the child did was kill the hawk. Then he decided to go into the village to kill his father and mother. On the way, he sang:

My mother gave birth to both of us,
She took Poko and abandoned Raôgo!
A giant hawk put me up in a tree:
I killed him!
A monkey took me down:
I killed him!
My village is a really big village,
but I will destroy it!

This is what he sang until he reached his father's compound.

When Poko saw Raôgo coming, she hid her mother in a large earthenware pot and her father in a granary.

Raôgo asked her:

1. This is a story of the terrible children, symbolizing social and cultural upheavals, and which also brings modernity into the society.

"Poko, where is your father?"
"My father is traveling."
"Poko, where is your mother?"
"My mother went to the pond."

Raôgo told her:

"Didn't my parents grow peanuts?"
"No!" said Poko.

Raôgo entered the mother's hut to look for peanuts. He opened the first pot and saw his mother hidden there. He killed her with one blow.

He left the hut and asked Poko:

"Is there anything in the granary?"
"No, it is empty!" Poko answered.
Raôgo went and opened the granary. He saw his father there whom he killed with one blow.

23

The Beautiful Daughter

A woman gave birth to a daughter who was very beautiful. She was so beautiful that she didn't want to give her away in marriage.

The day that her mother was to go to the market, she prepared some porridge for her daughter, gave her some flour as well, and advised her not to go to the pond when her friends came by.

When the woman had gone, around noon, the daughter's friends came and asked her to accompany them to the pond. She began to refuse but her friends convinced her to go.

They were bathing in the pond when a crocodile came out of the water. He stole their clothes and went back into the water.

The girls started to sing asking him to return their clothes to them.

One sang:

Handsome crocodile!
Handsome crocodile!
Give me back my skin!

The crocodile replied:

Pretty girl!
Pretty girl !
Come and get it!

The girl went to get her under garments. All the others did the same, and took back their clothing. Only the woman's beautiful daughter was left. She sang as well:

Handsome crocodile!
Handsome crocodile!
Give me back my skin!

And the crocodile told her:

Pretty girl!
Pretty girl!
Come and get it!

When she stepped into the pond, the crocodile pulled her down to the bottom of the water.

The woman came back from the market and did not find her daughter. She began to cry, while singing:

I gave birth to my daughter.
Her friends took her to the pond!
A crocodile caught her!

While she was singing, there was a turtledove nearby who was listening to her. The turtledove asked her:

"If I bring you back your daughter, what will you give me?"
"I will give you a plate of millet!"

The turtledove went and perched on a tree next to the pond. She began to sing:

Kuglguru, kuglguru, tumkugrwè[1]*!*
Kullu, Kullu gave birth!

1. Cooking of the turtledove

Kullu gave birth to a woman
who gave birth to a pretty daughter !
Kullu Ragoanna doesn't want her to marry,
Kullu Ragoanna !
Better to keep her and look at her
than give her away in marriage !
Kullu Ragoanna !

The crocodile heard the song, which pleased him. He said to the monitor lizard:

"Lizard, come watch over my daughter so that I can go listen to the song!"

The lizard accepted and the crocodile went out.

The turtledove sang again.

The lizard called the tortoise and asked her to come watch over the girl so that he could go listen to the song.

The lizard went out and the turtledove sang again.

The tortoise called the fish and asked him to come watch over the beautiful girl so that she could go listen to the song.

The fish accepted.

Soon, the dove sang again.

The fish went to see the frog and asked her to come watch over the beautiful girl so that he could go out and listen to the song.

When the frog arrived she, too, heard the turtledove's song, which pleased her.

She called the bullfrog and entrusted him with the girl's care. She also wanted to go out and hear the music.

When the frog had gone, the bullfrog heard the turtledove singing. He was enchanted by the music and asked the toad to come watch over the girl so that he could go listen to the song.

After the bullfrog left, the toad heard the song which pleased him. He asked the house to watch over the girl so that he could go listen to the song.

When the turtledove discovered that they were all outside and that the girl was alone, she went and got her, and took her back to her mother.

The crocodile returned and didn't find the girl.

He asked the monitor lizard:

"Lizard, who did you leave the girl with?"

"I left her with the tortoise so that she would watch her and I could go listen to the song," said the lizard.

"Tortoise, who did you leave the girl with?"

"I left her with the fish so that he would watch her and I could go listen to the song."

"Fish, who did you leave the girl with?"

"I left her with the frog so that she would watch her and I could go listen to the song."

"Frog, who did you leave the girl with?"

"I left her with the bullfrog so that he would watch her and I could go listen to the song."

"Bullfrog, who did you leave the girl with?"

"I left her with the toad so that he would watch her and I could go listen to the song."

"Toad, who did you leave the girl with?"

"I left her with the house so that it would watch her and I could go listen to the song."

The crocodile became angry.

He grabbed the toad and threw him on the ground.

The toad was injured, and was left a cripple.

This is why he hops instead of walks.

24

The Deceased Man's Possessions

An old man left on a journey. He went to a family to ask for hospitality. Unfortunately he soon fell ill. When he realized that he was going to die, he showed his host all of his possessions. He said to him:

"Here is all the wealth I have brought from home. If I die, take some of it for my funeral, and put the rest aside. If my family learns of my death and comes, you will give it to them for the orphans I leave behind."

The traveler died.

After the funeral washing the Muslims brought the defunct to the cemetery. When they had finished digging his grave, the host took the money, showed it to the people there and said that the defunct had asked that it be buried with his body, for he had no family.

The host took out a little for the funeral and the rest of it, that is, most of it, was buried with the old man. While they were closing up the grave, the host carefully watched the spot where the money was placed.

The night following the burial, the host came back to dig up the money. When he had finished digging, he reached out his hand to take the money but the corpse seized it and tore off its fingers.

This is how leprosy began in the world. It has its origin in dishonesty.

No one must take away an orphan's inheritance. He who does will come to a bad end.

25

The Story of a Woman and her Husband

A man lived with his wife. Each time he went out into the bush, he would bring something back. One day he brought back a bird and put it into a container which he closed with a lid. His wife was unaware of this; she opened the container and the bird escaped.

The man swore that he would beat the woman if she didn't find the bird. She looked for it with no success, and her husband beat her.

One day, the woman went to get water at the pond. There she found some small birds. She caught them, put them inside her earthenware jar and brought them home. Her spouse opened the container to drink some water and the birds escaped. The woman told him to do everything he could to find them.

He apologized but the wife wouldn't listen. So he finally went looking for them. He found them perched on a tree. When they saw the man, they began to sing:

Kî! Listen, children!
Kî! Listen, children!
One says that millet grows fast!
Another says there is a man walking;
One asks what he has come here for;
Another says that he flattered a woman at his house;
Another, that there is no one here who flatters women;
One said to fly away, and one flew away!
The other said to perch on top of the Caicedrat tree of Yèl[1]

1. The name of a village.

Another said that the Caicedrat tree fell down yesterday
And that the birds' eggs fell out
And that the birds' eggs fell out.

After singing, they went and perched on another tree. The man followed them. They sang again and flew farther on. The man continued following them, whereby he grew thirsty.

A turtledove saw him and went to perch on a tree near where he lived. She began to sing:

Kuglugluk, mother of Pug-Yende!
Kuglugluk, Kuglugluk!
Mother of Pug-Yende, kuglugluk !
You are at home, kuglugluk!
Pounding millet, Kuglugluk,
Your husband is in the bush, kuglugluk!
He is very thirsty, kuglugluk!

Pug-Yende said to her mother:

"Mother, do you hear what the bird is saying?"

Her mother accused the child of lying and threatened to beat her if she didn't go away.

The turtledove sang again. This time, the woman heard the song; she prepared a drink made from flour, and asked the turtledove to lead her to her husband. When she found him, he drank the flour water that she had brought him and the woman took him home.

This goes to show that if there is no forgiveness, the slightest thing becomes a problem. Men and women should listen to each other and forgive each other, or else they will never make a good match.

26

The Terrible Child

There was a child whose name was Yelkonlingma[1]. The village chief called to him one day and said:

"I have heard of your courage, but one day you will be surprised."

One day, on his way home from a walk he saw that the chief had sent his mother some millet so that she would prepare beer that day. His mother was in tears. He asked her why she was crying. She told him what the chief had asked her. He reassured her, saying it wasn't worth crying about. He went to get some stones. He brought them to the chief and asked him to open them up so that people could use them for drinking millet beer. So, the chief asked him:

"How can one open up stones for drinking beer?"

"And can anyone prepare beer in just one day?" answered the boy.

Annoyed, the chief ordered him to go away.

Another day, he again found his mother in tears. He asked her why she was crying. She told him that the chief had sent her a billy goat saying she should do everything she could to make it give birth. He reassured his mother and told her it wasn't worth crying about.

---

1. Literally: "I will never be surprised by a problem."

At nightfall, Yelkonlingma climbed up a tree and began cutting dead wood. The chief called to him and asked what he was doing in the tree. He replied:

"My father has just given birth, so I have come to get wood to heat the newborn baby's bath."

"How can a male give birth?" the chief exclaimed, offended.

"How could I know that a male cannot give birth? Didn't you send my mother a billy goat telling her to do everything she could so that he would give birth?" replied the child.

The chief again ordered him to go away since he was such a know-it-all.

This is how the mean and unjust chief came to leave Yelkonlingma's mother in peace.

27

The Liar's Tale

There was a liar who lived in a village. He died, leaving a son. The village chief called to the son and said to him:

"Your father spent his time lying in order to feed you. Now that he is dead, we will see how you get along!"

He replied that the lack of money could not kill him, for at his death his father had left him a horse whose dung was gold.

Meanwhile, he forced the horse to swallow a gold nugget.

The chief asked him to make his horse defecate, which he did by hitting him. A piece of gold was found in the horse's dung. The chief told the child to sell him his horse and he asked him the price he wanted for it. He told the chief that if he wanted to have the horse, he would first have to give him one hundred cows, one hundred donkeys, one hundred goats, and one hundred sheep.

The chief gave him everything he asked for and took the horse. He had a stable built in order to keep the horse locked up. He locked up the horse and waited for the stable to be full of golden turds, before letting it out.

When the stable was full of turds, the horse was let out. The chief demanded that the turds be washed, in order to find the gold.

But, no gold was found. Furious, the chief demanded that the liar's son be brought to him. Before arriving at the chief's house, the son killed a chicken. He took the blood, put it into the gizzard which he then tied around his mother's neck saying:

"When we arrive at the chief's, if he speaks to us, answer him rudely for I know what I'm going to do."

When they were at the chief's, the latter asked the boy for his animals back because the horse did not defecate any gold. At these words, the boy's mother told the chief that no one forced him to give his animals to her son. Just then, the son took his knife, and, as if seized by a sudden fury, cut the gizzard hanging from his mother's neck. The blood spurted out, and the mother fell down as if she were dead. The child took an animal's tail and whipped his mother's head and bottom with it and she stood up.

At this, the chief asked the boy how much he wanted for his tail. He asked for the same number of animals as the previous time. The chief accepted and the boy left with his mother.

One day as the chief was speaking, his favorite wife interrupted him. The chief, who didn't accept this from his wife, cut her throat.

When his servants asked him why he had struck his wife he replied that if it wasn't for them, he would finish her off.

He then took the tail and struck his wife's head and bottom in order to resuscitate her. But the woman remained still. He hit her again, but the poor woman's body was lifeless. He realized that the tail could not revive her. He ordered a bull to be killed and the stomach to be brought to him. He demanded that the liar's son be placed inside the stomach and thrown into a deep river. He had children carry it.

On the way to the river, the children met an animal which had hurt its paw. They put down the stomach in order to chase after it.

A man carrying a sack of gold happened to come by. When the liar's son heard his steps he began to talk to himself:

"Look here, for a gold nugget the chief had me trapped inside here so that I would be thrown into a gold mine."

When the passerby heard these words, he asked the boy to repeat them; then he said to him:

"I will get you out of there, and you, you will give me your place in the stomach so that I will be thrown into this gold mine!"

So the passerby entered the stomach and the liar's son left with the gold.

The children were unable to catch the injured animal. They came back and took up their load. They were saying:

"Everyday, everyday, you flatter the chief in order to eat! But your lie will be over today."

From the inside of the stomach, the passerby heard what the children were saying. He protested saying that he wasn't the liar's son, but the children threw him into the water.

The liar's son went back home. He dressed in the finest clothes and put the passerby's gold into his pocket. He took his horse and rode to the chief's house.

When the people saw him arrive, they hurried to tell the chief. The latter refused to believe that he had returned. The chief's favorite wife went to him and came back to tell her husband that it was indeed him. The chief also came out to see him. The liar's son greeted the chief and thanked him for having him thrown into a gold mine. He told the chief to bring him a calabash bowl so that he could offer him a bit of his gold. A bowl was brought to him, and he put some gold in it.

The chief couldn't stand still. He asked that one of his best bulls be killed and that he be put into its stomach. Then he asked the liar's son to throw him into the river.

No sooner said than done. The liar's son put him on his horse and went to throw him into the river.

Back in the village, this is what the boy announced to the chief's court:

"The chief said that he is content where he is. He's so happy there that he has no wish to come back, and he wants me to become chief in his place."

This is how the liar's son became chief of the village.

28

Poko and Raôgo Go Up To the Sky

A woman had twins, a girl named Poko and a boy named Raôgo.

One day she went to look for wood in the bush. She put the children down at the foot of a tree which she then climbed up. Unfortunately, she fell to her death.

A hawk took the children, brought them back to its nest, and raised them. The hawk gave the children these instructions:

"If you see a hawk coming towards you, know that it is I who is bringing you something to eat; but if you see a hawk coming from the east, kill it, for it is another hawk that is coming to take you away."

And he gave them a heavy iron club so they could defend themselves if necessary.

One day the father hawk went the wrong way. He returned home by the east, and the children killed him with the iron club. After the death of the father hawk, the children came down from the tree.

They decided to go where men lived. After walking for a long time, they found a chief sitting with his people. Raôgo asked Poko to go see what was happening. The chief was pleased to receive a visit from the beautiful children. He adopted them.

The day the chief and his family were out in the field, Raôgo told Poko that he was going to set fire to the palace. Poko advised him strongly against this, saying that the chief took care of them as he did his own children. Raôgo did not listen to her and set the palace on fire. From the field, the chief's family saw the fire and ran quickly home. Running, the chief said:

"My children, my beautiful foreign children, what will become of them?"

Just when the whole palace was covered in flames, Raôgo and Poko climbed up into a Kapok tree. When the chief arrived home, he did not find them. He thought they had died in the fire, and he wanted to hang himself. The people calmed him, had him sit down, and consoled him. Sitting under the Kapok tree, he went on crying.

Then Raôgo told Poko that he was going to relieve himself on the chief. Poko tried to dissuade him because of the suffering the chief was going through at their disappearance.

Despite all that, Raôgo relieved himself and sullied the chief. The latter raised his head and saw the children up in the tree. He ordered the tree to be cut, so that his enemies would have to come down.

He was deeply hurt for he would never have thought that the children could set fire to his palace, since he had always considered them as his own children.

So the blacksmiths were called to chop down the Kapok tree. When the tree was about to fall a salamander crawled out of a hole and cried: *ko! ko! ko!* The trunk of the tree became all smooth again, as if it had never been cut.

Raôgo told Poko that he was going to eat the salamander. Poko advised him against this, saying that if he ate it, the tree would fall over and they would be captured. But Raôgo did not listen to her. He seized the salamander and cut off its head. He gave the head to Poko, telling her to put it in her cheek, and he ate the rest.

Meanwhile, the blacksmiths went back to cutting down the Kapok tree. When the tree was about to fall, the head of the salamander that was in Poko's cheek cried: *ko! ko! ko!* and the tree returned to the way it was. But Raôgo took the head out of Poko's cheek and ate it.

The blacksmiths went on with their work, the tree fell, and the children died.

The chief ordered their bodies to be thrown away without being buried. So, they were thrown away. But, mysterious things were about to happen!

When those who had thrown away the bodies turned around, Raogo and Poko stood up and set off on their way.

They saw another group of people. Raôgo told Poko to take a detour in order to go and ask the people what was going on.

When they approached the group, they were told:

"There is a huge hawk that swoops down here every seven days to swallow people up. Today we have decided to gather together so that he will come and swallow each of us, once and for all, so that finally we will have peace and quiet."

Raôgo reassured them:

"Come now, go back to your homes and your families, and leave him to me!"

Soon the hawk flew down onto a rock which was stuck in the ground. He opened his beak and fire came out of it. He approached Raôgo. The latter took the iron club that he had used to kill the first hawk, and he struck him. The hawk fell, but got up again. He hit him once more. He fell and got back up. In the end, he succeeded in killing the giant hawk.

The inhabitants rejoiced. They told Raôgo to ask for anything he wanted as a reward. He told them he wanted the sky. Blacksmiths were called upon, who worked for twenty days. But the ladder they built didn't reach as high as the sky. Other blacksmiths were called in, who worked for one hundred days. Finally, Raôgo was able to go up to the sky, and he helped his sister Poko climb up as well.

Today, they are the ones who are up in the sky and who make such a racket.

Raogo goes : *wuruwuru*[1] !

Poko asks him to stop, for there are children of men on earth.

But Raôgo outdoes himself, exclaiming:

"Do I have a wife or child on earth? *Worr ! Woss*[2] !

1. Roaring of thunder.
2. Noise of the storm accompanied by rain.

29

The World Turns, The World Changes

Back when slavery still existed, a rich man named Runiwangda bought a slave whose name was Runigilgda, "the world turns." When they arrived home, he asked him:

"What did you used to do?"
"Business," he answered.

The rich man provided him with some money so that he could do business. The slave started his business and earned a lot of money.

But one night when Runigilgda was thinking things over in his head, he felt overcome with sadness: when he had left his home, his father was so old that it had been his job to support his family.

At sunrise, he went to see his master and told him what was worrying him:

"It's been twelve years since I left my home. At that time, my father was already very old and I was made head of the family. Now, I don't know what is happening with them. This is why I have come to see you. If a slave can buy back his freedom, I have the means to do it. I would like to return to my family."

Runigilgda did, in fact, have the money for when he was running his business he had saved up twenty-five francs a day.

After listening to him, his master agreed to set him free. Runigilgda asked him how much he should pay him to regain his freedom. His master asked for the amount of money he had given him to start his business. Runigilgda paid it back to him and thanked his master who, for the last twelve years had taken care of him as he would his own son. He had treated him with respect and had never mistreated him.

When Runigilgda returned home, the village chief had been dead for a long time. But nobody had yet taken his place.

The population came out to greet him. The rich people gave him presents which he distributed to the needy. Thus the people could tell he was not only rich but above all he was generous. So they named him chief of the village.

Meanwhile, Runiwangda, his former master, had fallen into slavery. He was led from one marketplace to another, but no one wanted him because he was too old. Seeing that no one came forward to buy Runiwangda, someone suggested to the seller to go see Runigilgda, because he would surely buy Runiwangda and keep him in his court. He would not make him suffer. He was sure of it. So the seller led Runiwangda to the chief Runigilgda. The chief recognized the prisoner immediately. He asked him:

"Do you know me?"

He said no. He asked the question three times, but the prisoner kept saying no. The chief introduced himself. He bought old Runiwangda and kept him in his court.

When the seller had gone, the chief gave the old man one hundred sheep, one hundred heads of cattle, and one hundred goats. He had a house built for him and gave him wives.

Runiwangda again became like a chief.

This tale advises us to be careful, for the world is always turning. You can be rich one day and become poor the next, or come to a bad end.

He who is rich today must therefore help the others for we know what today has in store for us, but we don't know what tomorrow will bring.

30

Sombé[1]

An old man had two wives. The first was sterile. The second one gave birth to a boy. The old man spent all night wondering what name to give his son. When day came, he discussed the problem with his first wife, who told him to name him Sombé. So the child was named Sombé.

A few years later the second wife died, and the old man as well. Only Sombé and the first wife were left.

The latter wondered what she could do to defeat Sombé. She got an idea. She found a large field and ordered the young man to work there all alone, sowing and harvesting. Sombé agreed.

Sombé had a dog. Every day he left it at home so he could go into the field. When he had gone, his step-mother prepared some porridge[2] and put poison into the sauce to kill him. The dog, having seen the step-mother do this, ran to join his master in the field and warn him. He said to him:

"When you get home if your step-mother offers you some porridge, refuse to eat it and ask her to prepare you some beans, for she put some poison in the sauce to kill you."

When he arrived home, the woman busied herself all around him, greeted him and gave him something to eat. Sombé refuse the food and asked her for some beans. She eventually went and prepared some for him.

---

1. Literally: "He who is good."
2. A dish made of millet or corn which is eaten with a sauce. It is the daily staple of the Moose people, *sagbo*, in Moore.

The next day, once he had gone to the field, she prepared a sauce with beans and put some poison in it. The dog went and told his master about it.

When he arrived home Sombé refused the sauce with beans and asked for some porridge.

The next day when he had gone, the step-mother prepared some porridge and some beans and added poison. The dog ran to warn his master about it and told him to ask for some *zom koom*[3]. The old woman eventually ground some flour to prepare *zom koom* for Sombé.

The step-mother learned later that the dog was the one informing his master. So she made the decision to kill Sombé directly.

That day when he left for the field, the dog went with him and told him that he should no longer return home or else the old woman would kill him.

Together, they went down the road without knowing where to go. They arrived at the entrance to a village. The dog asked Sombé to kill him and bury him. Sombé refused. The dog insisted and finally Sombé did what he had asked.

When he arrived in the village, the chief had just died and the people were getting ready to bury him. Sombé offered to help them. When they were looking for a new chief, someone suggested Sombé.

Ever since Sombé had left his step-mother's house, she suffered from hunger and had no one to take care of her. So one day she decided to leave.

She arrived at the entrance to a village and lay down next to a well. When the women of the village came to get water, she told them she was hungry and asked them for something to eat. The women gave her water and said they had nothing there for her to eat.

Once they were back in the village, the women told the chief. He gave them some peanuts and asked them to place them on the ground, one by one, until they reached the well.

---

3. Literally: "flour water." It is the drink offered to guests to welcome them.

The women did what he had asked. When they had finished drawing water from the well, the old woman saw a peanut and took it. A little farther off she saw another one. She followed each one of the peanuts until she reached the doors of the palace.

When the chief saw her, he recognized her. He asked her:

"Do you recognize me?"

She said no. He asked her the question three times, and three times she said no. So the chief told her:

"I am your son, Sombé."

The old woman was so afraid she didn't know what to do with herself. But the chief consoled her and had a house built for her within the walls of his palace.

He took care of her as he would his own mother.

This is why everyone is asked to be good, instead of hurting one another and then being ashamed of it, afterwards.

31

A Fruitful Investment

One day, some Yarse[1] arrived at a village where princes were waiting to steal from them. They found the population at work. Some were weaving skirts, others were weaving mats. They gave a few kola nuts to a child, telling him:

"Give them to the old men of the village who are sitting there."

The child did so, and the old men said to the merchants:

"Wait, don't leave!"

The old men informed them that princes were lying in wait on the road to steal from them, and they hid the foreigners.

The princes waited for their victims in vain, and left.

The old men said to themselves:

"The lucky man's belt breaks near the vine[2]. If the Yarse hadn't had any consideration for us, we would have let them be attacked."

This is why it is said that one kola nut alone can save the whole sack.

It is also said that in order to have a thousand kolas, you need to spend a gourd-full.

1. Muslim weaver merchants whose principal occupation is caravan trading.

2. Proverb that can be adapted in today's world as: "The lucky man's car breaks down near a garage."

32

How the Yarse and the Guinea-Fowl Became Enemies

There were Yarse who left for war in the company of other Yarse. At that time, all the villages were at war. On their way, they became thirsty. They met Issaka, a guinea-fowl, and asked him:

"Where did you find water to drink?"

He told them that there was no more water when he got there, only mud left, and that was what he had used. The place he was talking about was rather far away. The chief of the Yarse asked him:

"Can you take us there?"

He refused, and the leader of the expedition said to him:

"Father Issaka, you too, are Muslim like us. It's just that we are Yarse and your name is Issaka. What is the difference?"

The guinea-fowl still refused.

They left him there and continued on their way. They came upon a warthog. He too had gone to look for water and had to settle for mud. The chief of the Yarse asked him:

"Where did you find water, dear friend?"

"Truthfully, when I got to the river there was no more water. I sucked the mud and I rolled in it to refresh myself. Can't you see that my body is still wet?" replied the warthog.

"Can you take us there?" the Yarse asked.

He willingly agreed.

He led them to the river.

The chief of the Yarse asked them to sit down for a moment while they prayed that God would give them water.

The Yarse chief prayed and the river filled with water. They drank, washed, and even filled their gourds.

Then the chief of the Yarse said to the warthog:

"I have nothing to offer you, but I give you the river. She belongs to you. If you see someone lurking around and you are the stronger, then chase him away for the river is yours. And if Issaka the guinea-fowl comes to the river, catch him, pluck him, hit him with burning branches until he becomes completely red, then cut his throat. Even though he followed God's law for a thousand years, when he found us in difficulty, we his Muslim brothers, he did not even take pity on us. This is why I tell you to hit him with burning branches, to kill him and to cut off his head."

This is why nowadays, even though the guinea-fowl himself practices fasting on the last day of Ramadan, the Muslim cuts his throat to celebrate the breaking of the fast. Even if there are ten chickens around him, he is the one that the Yarse will kill, because he refused to help his ancestors who nearly died of thirst.

It is also because of this story that the Yarse decided to no longer eat the meat of the warthog, because of the help he gave to their ancestors. Nor do the Yarse eat pork because he is of the same family as the warthog, except that he lives in the bush.

33

The Origin of Joking Relationships between the Poɛɛse, Yarse, and Peuls

There were two Poɛɛse[1] who were born the same day, one in the morning, the other in the evening. When it came time for them to marry, they both desired the same girl. The one born in the morning said that he would be the one to marry the girl; he who was born in the evening swore it would be him.

So a fight broke out between them. They chased after each other and one of them went down a hole. He was very lucky because when he went down the hole, a spider, who was spinning her web, closed up the entrance.

When the second one got to the edge of the hole he found a Peul[2] and a Yarga[3] sitting there drinking milk. They had seen the man who had gone into the hole. When the second one asked if anybody had passed that way the Peul wanted to say yes, but the Yarga motioned for him to keep quiet. So he was silent.

The Poɛɛga told the Peul not to be afraid to say anything about what he had seen. The Peul told him to dig in the hole and look inside. He dug in the hole and killed his rival.

1. The Poɛɛse constitute a social group which lives at the court where it is responsible for trials by ordeals. Subgroup of the Moaaga ethnic group. Singular: A Poɛɛga.

2. Breeder of livestock. Nomadic herdsmen also known as Fulani, found in several areas of West, Central, and East Africa.

3. Muslim tradesman.

The Yarga insulted the Peul and called him good-for-nothing. Why did he get the man killed? He also insulted the Poεεga who had murdered his brother.

This is how the joking relationship began between the Poεεga, the Yarga and the Peul. Even today when they meet each other, they have fun insulting one another.

But no one insults mothers.

34

Other People's Faults

A Peul lived in the bush with his wife, his son, and his livestock. They had no neighbors. One day the man and his wife went out. Only the child was left at home.

An old man came and found the child and asked him where his parents were. He answered that they had both gone out.

A bull, a cow, and a calf were tied up in the yard.

The old man asked the child:

"If your bull dies, what will you do?"

"My mother and I will take it to my father who will cut it up," the child answered him.

"And if the cow dies, what will you do?" the old man asked again.

"My mother and I will take it to my father who will cut it up," answered the child.

He asked again:

"And if the calf dies, what will you do?"

"My mother and I will take it to my father to cut it up," answered the child.

The old man laughed and said to the child:

"If your father returns, tell him that an old man came by but it wasn't for a quarrel."

That evening the father came home and the child gave him the message. The father told his son that in fact it wasn't a quarrel, but a piece of advice:

"Here is what the questions mean:

We are alone here. If I die, what will you do? I am the bull. If I die, who will dig the grave?

And if your mother dies, what will we do? Your mother is the cow.

And you, if you die, what will we do? You are the calf.

In conclusion, the old man is giving us a piece of advice. He advises us to join the other members of the village."

Thus, the Peul went to live near a group of three dwellings. When he had finished moving in, he realized that the inhabitants of the three dwellings each had a serious fault. One was a rapist, the other a thief, and the third a slanderer[1].

One day while the Peul was sitting down, he saw the old man coming. He told him:

"I followed your advice and I moved, but I still have problems. I would still like to go somewhere else."

The old man told him not to move again, for what he thought were problems, were really not. He was convinced and he stayed.

Meanwhile the thief grew old and stopped stealing. The rapist grew old and stopped raping. The slanderer also grew old. He was bedridden and could no longer go out but his fault did not stop.

This is to tell us that some faults disappear with age, but not slander. If people who got along well end up hating one another, keep in mind that someone has turned them against each other.

The world moves like a tree.

All the troubles found in it are caused by slanderers.

1. *Munafika.* This is a man who stirs up bad feelings between people. The slanderer is hated by the Moose.

35

Bibêga, the Terrible Child

There was a pregnant woman. She went into the bush to look for wood. A thorn pricked her in the belly. The child came out and asked her:

"Mother, do you know what my name is?"
"I don't know," answered the mother.
"Well! My name is Bibêga! Let's go home, do not be afraid!"

His mother brought him home.
Some time later he asked her if there wasn't another fearless person in the village.
He asked the same question in a place where there were children. The latter told him that they too, were afraid of nothing. He asked them to accompany him on an adventure.
They arrived at the home of a chief and asked him to put them up for the night. The latter had some porridge[1] prepared for them and asked that an animal be killed for his guests.
When night fell, Bibêga told his companions that he wanted to go and chat for a while with some girls. The chief had three girls come over for he thought they liked one another.
In the course of the evening, the girls fell asleep. Bibêga told his companions that he was going to kill his girl. They tried to dissuade him. After all, the chief had given them hospitality, had brought them girls for the night, and had treated them well. Why did he want to kill the girl he had taken? He told them:

---

1. Dish made from millet or corn flour, eaten daily by the Moose, *sagbo* in Moore.

"I am going to kill her, but I didn't ask you to do the same."

He killed her, as well as the two others.

His companions ran off.

He climbed a tree in front of the compound and signaled their disappearance. He had them hunted down with no success after alerting the whole village with the sound of his drum.

From up in the tree, Bibêga defecated into the flour water[2] which the chief had asked for to quench his thirst. The chief looked up and saw him sitting in the tree. He alerted the population, for he had found his enemy.

People arrived and began cutting down the tree. Right when the tree was about to fall, a long-crested eagle[3] came and asked the boy what was going on. He told him that they were chopping down the tree in order to kill him. The bird told him:

"If that is the case, then come under my wings!"

He did so and the bird flew off with him.

When they reached the top of a rock, he told the bird that he was going to cut off one of his wings and draw water with it. He cut one of his wings off and they both fell to their deaths.

The tortoise came along and wondered how on earth both of them could have died. She said:

"If there was gratitude on earth, I would do something good for you."

---

2. *Zom koom* in Moore.

3. *Lophaetus occipitalis* (Accipitridae).

She went and fetched some water and splashed it on them. They were both resuscitated. And Bibêga exclaimed:

"A tortoise ! A tortoise !"
The eagle said to him:
"She saved us and you want to kill her?"

He said:

"I am going to kill my tortoise, but I didn't ask you to do the same."
He killed it, cooked it over a grill, ate it, and continued on his way.

He went and found an old woman who was working in her okra field. He told her:

"Dear madam, let me help you !"

The old woman accepted his help and said:

"I am going home to pound some millet and I will bring you back some water to drink."

So she left for her home. As she was returning to the field, she met Bibêga, who was coming to join her at her house. He told the old woman that he wanted something hot to eat because he had been out a long time.
They went back to the house. The old woman prepared a sauce and took some flour to make porridge. When she began to stir the porridge, Bibêga seized her and plunged her head into the cooking pot. Then he went on his way.

He went and found a blacksmith in his shop and said to him:

"Dear sir, let me help you!"

The blacksmith accepted his help. He went to lie down and fell asleep.

Bibêga killed him and ran off.

36

The Donkey Thieves

There were two thieves.

At nightfall, they stopped next to a man's compound. They were looking for a way to get in to steal the man's donkey.

They decided to separate in order to execute their plan. Then, they would find each other again with a whistle signal.

Meanwhile, the man was in the process of relieving himself in the bushes near his courtyard, and he heard them.

One of the thieves entered the courtyard and began to untie the donkey. The man came after him with an axe. In the dark, the thief thought it was his companion.

The donkey owner struck the thief in the back. He left the donkey and ran off.

The man then hid himself in the dark, and whistled. The thief who had tried to untie the donkey came to meet him. Again he thought he had met up with his companion. The donkey owner asked him:

"Didn't you untie him?

"No," he answered, "and what is more, its owner took me by surprise and struck me on the back with an axe."

The man asked him to come closer so that he could see his injury. He took this opportunity to strike him again. The thief again ran off. He passed the other thief who signaled to him by whistling. Thinking that it was still the owner of the donkey, he said to him:

"Your mother ! Your mother ! Your mother !"[1]

And thus ends this tale, which says that it is dangerous to steal the goods of another.

1. A very serious insult which uses the name of the mother.

37

The Chief, the Hawk, the Turtledove, and the Little Child

One day, a chief sat resting under a tree in his courtyard. He saw a hawk chasing a turtledove. The turtledove flew into the chief's pocket, and the hawk perched on his shoulder. The turtledove said to the chief:

"If you save me from the hawk, you will have all that you desire on earth."

The hawk said to the chief:

"If you hand the turtledove over to me all of your sterile wives will have children."

The chief sat, perplexed. He didn't know what to do.

Meanwhile, a group of children came and sat next to him. One of them, who had noticed his demeanor, asked him point-blank:

"How can a hawk perched on your shoulder make you so perplexed?"

The chief explained his predicament to the children.

Another child made the following suggestion to the chief:

"Ask the hawk if he prefers to eat meat, or a turtledove!"

When the chief asked the hawk the question, he replied that he felt like eating meat.

So the child told the chief to have a ram killed, to cut it up, and to give it to him.

The chief did this.

When he had eaten his fill, the hawk said to the chief:

"Look! Your well that is situated behind your courtyard will never dry up. If you drink its water, you will have many children."

After the hawk left, the turtledove came out and said to the chief:

"God willing, everything that you desire on this earth, you will have."

She also left.

So in this tale, the child is the one who finds the answer to the chief's problem. This teaches us that when old people speak, children must also be allowed to have their say.

38

The Children of the Brave Woman

A bachelor was living in his village. During this time he married a young girl who only gave birth to daughters whereas all of the other women in the village gave birth to sons.

The woman, unhappy at having only girls, insulted her husband, her family, the entire village.

An old man of the village, aware of this, decided to give some advice to the woman who was insulting everyone. He had her come to him and told her not to take it out on the population. If she had no child at all, it could be said that it was because her husband was sterile. But if she had only girls, it was God's will.

In spite of the old man's advice, the woman spoke badly to him. He told her this:

"What you see there before you is a shrine[1]. If you ask it for something, you will receive it. If you want to go see it, go in the morning or in the evening, but not at noontime whatever you do, for that is when its children are out."

Deep down, woman did not believe the old man's words. She said to herself:

1. *Tenkugri*, a sacred place inhabited by the souls of the ancestors.

"Why will the shrine's children be out at noontime, instead of resting?"

She decided to go see the shrine at noon. She took a chicken and asked that it be offered as a sacrifice so that she would give birth to sons.

A few months later she became pregnant and gave birth to a boy.

She became pregnant a second time and gave birth to a boy.

Unfortunately, both of them were retarded.

One day, their father sent them to get his goat which was at their uncle's house. The uncle put a rope around the animal's neck and gave it to them.

Before they arrived home, the goat was lost. This is what they said to each other:

"Where is the goat?"
"Weren't you the one leading it?"
"Weren't you the one pushing it from behind?"

This teaches us that we must not doubt the words of an older person.

There is in fact a proverb which says:

"An old person's mouth may smell, but his words do not."

39

An Orphan Girl Must Not be Mistreated[1]

There was a woman who died leaving her daughter with her husband's other wife. One day, this woman made some sorghum beer. Her husband drank a little of it and also gave some to his daughter. But when the little girl drank, her spit touched the gourd. The stepmother told the girl that this gourd could not be washed at home, but only in the river Lê-Lê.

The child took the gourd and started down the road singing:

My wicked mother, my wicked mother
prepared some sorghum beer.
My father served me some of it,
my spit touched her gourd.
She says her gourd cannot be washed here,
but only in the Lê-Lê.

While she was walking along singing this song, she met an old woman who was washing herself. The woman asked her to scrub her back. She willingly accepted and scrubbed the old lady's back, who then wished her a safe journey.

On her way she found some porridge[2] and some sauce on the side of the road. The porridge invited her to eat it.

---

1. An orphan girl receives divine protection and she can bring great misfortunes upon those who would do her harm.
2. Daily meal of the Moose made from millet flour or corn flour, *sagbo* in Moore.

She said:

"Who ate me, that I should eat you"?

The porridge wished her a safe journey.

Farther on, she met an old woman who had left her house after spreading her okra outside her door to dry. It began to rain so the girl brought the okra into the house and sat down. A little while later, the old woman returned home in the rain and asked:

"Who is the good child inside my house?"

"A bad girl is inside!" answered the girl.

"Do you want me to put you into a granary full of gold?" asked the old woman.

"Put me wherever you wish," said the child.

So she put her in a granary full of silver, and she gave her a gourd full of grain to pound.

"If a bird insults you, do not insult it!"

The girl took the gourd and began to pound.

The bird insulted her; she was silent and continued to pound.

Then the old woman told her to come out. When she came out, cattle, sheep, horses and goats followed her. The old woman offered them to her as a gift.

The orphan girl returned home with her riches.

When she arrived home her stepmother was jealous of her. She told her husband to draw some beer from the earthenware pot, to drink it, and to give some of it to her own child[3]. The latter sullied the gourd with her spit. So her mother took this opportunity to ask her to go wash the gourd in the river.

---

3. That is, to the half-sister of the orphan girl.

The child obeyed and went down the road to the river. Like the orphan girl, she came upon an old woman who was washing herself. The old woman asked her to scrub her back. She replied in an insolent manner:

"I don't even scrub my own mother's back, and you are telling me to scrub yours?"

The old woman cursed her.

She continued on her way. She then found some porridge and some sauce on the side of the road. The porridge told her to eat it. She sat down and ate it all. The porridge cursed her.

Afterwards, she found some okra spread out by an old woman in front of her door, just as it was starting to rain. She took shelter inside the old woman's house and left the okra out in the rain. When the old woman came back, she asked:

"Who is the bad child inside my house?"

"It's a good girl inside!" the girl replied.

The old woman gave her a gourd and asked her to pound its contents, adding,

"If a bird insults you, don't insult it!"

When she began to pound, the bird insulted her and she insulted it back.

The old woman asked her:

"Do you want me to put you into a granary full of silver, or a granary full of gold?"

She told her to put her into a granary full of gold.

She was put inside, but was eaten. All that was left was her skull.

The bird picked it up and took it back to her house, singing:

Sweep the courtyard well, for Tar-Ma[4] *is coming!*
Sweep the courtyard well, for Tar-Ma is coming!
Sweep the courtyard well for Tar-Ma is coming!

When the bird arrived, it found the courtyard very clean; it dropped the skull into the middle of it.

And the mother began to cry.

That is why it is advised not to mistreat an orphan girl.

---

4. Literally: "She who has a mother."

40

There Is Always Someone Cleverer Than You, Somewhere

There were two childhood friends. The wife of one of them gave birth to a daughter that he gave away in marriage to the other. This one decided to move to a different village, for he said:

"I don't wish to remain in the village where she was born for fear that someone else might desire her."

So he went away and he built a new house where he put the girl. He did not want another man to see her. He even dug latrines inside of the house so that she wouldn't have to go outside to relieve herself.

But the young girl had a suitor in her village. One day, the young man decided to go look for her. He made inquiries and started off for the village where his beloved was being held. When he arrived there, an old woman warned him that his job wouldn't be easy, and she demanded the sum of fifty thousand francs[1]. The young man immediately gave her the amount she asked for.

The old woman told him:

"Go into the bush and build a canoe big enough for you to fit inside and bring it back to me!"

---

1. Or 76.3 euros, a considerable sum locally.

The young man did as he was told.

The old woman put him into the canoe and packed him tightly in with ropes. Then she asked for help carrying her *fêdo*[2] which she wanted to entrust to someone.

So the old woman had the canoe brought to the house of the young woman's husband and said to him:

"Since I must go away on a short trip, I have come to entrust you with my canoe. Store it in your house!"

The man had the canoe brought into his house. Soon afterwards, the young suitor untied his ropes and got out of the small boat. He thus found himself in the company of the man's wife.

Three days later, the old woman returned for her canoe. She had help bringing it home. The young man climbed out and went home.

About ten days later, the young man came back. He again befriended the old woman. She again put him into the small boat, which some children carried to the home of the jealous husband. When they arrived at his house, the man had them set the canoe down on the ground outside. He told the old lady that he would later store it inside his house.

When the old woman was gone, the husband's young brothers told him that they found her strange, and that they didn't trust her. They wanted to unpack the canoe to see what was inside. The man didn't see the need for this, but his brothers insisted. As soon as they opened it up, the lover jumped out and ran away. They chased after him in vain.

The old woman moved to another village.

This is why one mustn't sequester one's wife, for that could bring bad surprises.

---

2. Empty container.

41

The Old Woman and her Daughters

An old woman had daughters who were getting too old for marriage. No one came to ask for their hand because their mother didn't want to see any man at her house.

However, one man had an idea. One day when the wind had started to blow and it was about to rain, he decided to go by the old woman's door. The latter said to him:

"Dear child, instead of running, come inside my house and get out of the rain!"

The man told her:

"I'm sorry, but I have daughters at home ! They are all virgins and I heard that today the wind will blow away all the virgin girls. This is why I'm running, in order to save them!"

The old woman cried and begged the man to come help her, for she had two virgin girls at home.

The man entered the house and found the two girls. When he had finished deflowering them he went out and wanted to leave. The old woman told him:

"Dear child, do not leave! It's been a long time since I had a man!"

The man told her:

"You're on your own!"

And he left.

42

The Two Wives

A man had two wives. When he gave them the money they needed to buy food, each of them received one thousand francs. Thus, being financially equal, each of them had the same amount with which to do the cooking. The master of the house was pleased the day his first wife was going to cook, but when it came time for the second wife to cook it was a catastrophe. Her name was Mamounata. The head of the household said to her:

"Mamounata, you are the one who again prepared this disgusting meal? What am I to do with you? I give both of you the same amount of money for the market! But I'm beginning to wonder if you're not using this money for yourself!"

This is how the husband reprimanded Mamounata whereas in fact, she was the victim of the first wife's jealousy. Indeed, when Mamounata was preparing her sauce, the first wife took the opportunity when she was out of the kitchen to come and urinate into the cooking pot, so that not even flavoring made from seeds of the Néré tree could give the sauce the right taste.

Every day when Mamounata was cooking, it was the same thing, so that the husband's friends who ate with him advised him to repudiate her because she was tarnishing the family reputation.

Hopeless, and at the end of her rope, Mamounata went to confide in an old woman who promised to shed some light on the situation in order to save her home. The old woman told her:

"Go to the market and spend all the money your husband gives you on food. Then, prepare the sauce. But before going to draw water from the pond with your earthenware jar, put the cooking pot on the fire with a good amount of shea butter and put the lid on the pot."

Mamounata did what the old woman said.

Right when she was about to go draw water, the first wife said to her:

"Don't worry! I will watch your sauce for you!"

When she had gone, the first wife hurried over to the sauce and squatted down over the pot to urinate. At the first squirt of urine the pot caught fire and burnt her genitals.

She ran into the bedroom and rubbed herself with butter to relieve the pain, but nothing happened!

When Mamounata returned, she found her in a very sad state and asked what she was suffering from. She didn't want to tell her anything. She called for her husband but he was still at work.

When she heard the sound of his moped she ran to the door to beg him to come see what was wrong with her. The husband joined her in the bedroom and she showed him her wound. She was taken to the hospital right away and was cared for.

From this day on, she never again dared to harm the second wife, Mamounata.

This is why the Moose say:

F sâ tubs gnîgri, f tubsa f gnôg zugu!

"He who spits in the air receives the spit on his chest"; or again :

Sâan putoog ned n gnûda a bînd koom!
"The host with bad intentions ends up drinking his own urine and excrement."

He who harms others always ends up being punished for his bad actions.

Short Bibliography for Further Reading

Delobsom, A. A. Dim. *L'Empire du Mogho-Naba, coutumes des Mossi de la Haute-Volta.* [The Mogho-Naba Empire; Mossi Customs in Upper Volta]. (Preface by Robert Randau). Paris : Editions Domat-Montchréstien, 1932. 303 p.

Houis, Maurice. *Les noms individuels chez les Mossi.* Dakar : IFAN, 1963. 141 p.

Ilboudo, Pierre. *Croyances et pratiques religieuses traditionnelles des Mossi.* [Beliefs and Traditional Religious Practices of the Mossi]. Paris and Ougadougou : CNRS and CVRS, 1966. 112 p. (Recherches voltaïques, no. 3.)

Izard, Michel. *Introduction à l'histoire des royaumes Mossi*, 2 vols. Paris and Ouagadougou : CNRS and CVRS, 1970. 432 p. (Recherches voltaïques, nos. 12 and 13.) (Paris: Laboratoire d'anthropologie sociale, Collège de France, 1970).

——. *Le Yatenga précolonial: un ancient royaume du Burkina.* [Pre-colonial Yatenga : a former kingdom of Burkina]. Paris : Karthala, 1985. 164 p.

——. "The Peoples and Kingdoms of the Niger Bend and the Volta Basin from the 12th to the 16th Century." In *General History of Africa*, Vol. 4, edited by D.T. Niane, pp. 211-237. Berkeley and Los Angeles: University of California Press, 1984.

Ki-Zerbo, Joseph. *Histoire de l'Afrique noire d'hier à demain.* Paris : Hatier, 1972. 708p. 2nd ed. 1978. 731 p.

McFarland, Daniel M. and Rupley, Lawrence A., eds. *Historical Dictionary of Burkina Faso.* Lanham, Md., and London : Scarecrow Press, 1998. 2nd ed. 279 p. (African Historical Dictionaries, No. 74).

Merlet, Annie. *Textes anciens sur le Burkina Faso* (1853-1897). Paris and Ouagadougou : Sépia/ADDB, 1995. 294p. (Coll. Découvertes du Burkina.)

Sissao, Alain-Joseph. *La littérature orale moaaga comme source d'inspiration de quelques romans burkinabè.* [Oral moaaga literature as a source of inspiration for a few burkinabè novels]. Doctoral thesis. Université de Paris XII Val-de-Marne, 2 vols., 1995. 732 p.

Skinner, Elliott Percival. *The Mossi of the Upper Volta: The Political Development of a Sudanese People.* Stanford, Calif.: Stanford University Press, 1964. [Reprinted as the Mossi of Burkina Faso, Prospect Heights, Illinois: Waveland Press, 1989].

Tiendrébéogo, Yamba. *Histoire et coutumes royales des Mossi de Ouagadougou.* [History and Royal Customs of the Mossi of Ouagadougou]. Edited by Robert Pageard. Ouagadougou: chez le Larhallé Naba, Presses Africaines, 1964. 205 p.